SHALLCROSS
Animal Slippers

Charles Porter

Illustrated by Kathy Von Ertfelda, Loxahatchee FL. Cover art by Gisela Pferdekamper, Loxahatchee FL. Cover design by Paula Batchelor. Interior design and formatting by Paula Batchelor (Spectrum Marketing Group); New Bedford, MA.

charlesporterauthor.com

Library of Congress Cataloging-in-Publication Data
Porter, Charles
Library of Congress Control Number: 2020900137
   Charles Porter, Loxahatchee, FL
ISBN: 978-0-9894256-4-3 (trade paper)
ISBN: 978-0-9894256-5-0 (ePub)

Printed in the United States of America

"You can't offend nature."
– Triple Suiter

*"My mind leads me to speak now of forms
changed into new bodies."*
– Ovid, Metamorphoses

For Charles Porter, Florida Boy

-Aubrey Shallcross

Contents

PART THREE

ATLANTIC OCEAN

FLORIDA

Jacksonville
Jacksonville Beach

Gainesville

Saint Johns R.

Crescent Lake

Lake George

Saint Johns R.

Daytona Beach

Tsala Apopka Lake

Orlando

Cape Canaveral

Melbourne
Palm Bay

Clearwater
Largo
Tampa
Saint Petersburg

Lake Kissimmee

Indian River

Tarpon Bay

Sarasota

Port
Saint Lucie

Area of The
Dragon and
Two-toed Tom

Lake Okeechobee

West Palm
Beach

Charlotte Harb.

Pine Island

Cape Coral

Delray Beach
Boca Raton
Pompano Beach

Sanibel Island

Coral Springs

Fort Lauderdale
Hollywood, Florida

Big Cypress Swamp

Cape Romano

The Everglades

Hialeah
Miami

Biscayne Bay

Cape Sable

Key Largo
Key Largo

Florida Bay

Islamorada

Dry Tortugas
Loggerhead Key

Marquesas Keys

Gull Keys

Marathon

Key West

Florida Keys

Straits of Florida

x

Introduction

This is a series. The third book. Background from the previous two books Shallcross and Flame Vine could improve your appreciation of its content. Maybe. Up to you.

The Shallcross novels are: Florida, film, music, love, history, religion, crime, country, horses, and decades of Rolling Stone. They are American stadium, for fifty years of Aubrey Shallcross's life. Aubrey is a voice hearer, as are people in populations everywhere; other words for this are "audio hallucinations" or "schizophrenia." Aubrey has heard Triple Suiter's voice in his mind since he was very young, yet he, like a lot of voice hearers, appears normal and is afraid to tell anyone lest he be considered mentally ill. These voices are called "slippers." No one has ever been able to explain their origin. Science implies that the brain manufactures them, but science is silent as to how or where in the brain they are created. What if the voices are separate from the brain and just live there? What if they are surviving spirits, the revenants of those who have died, left their corporeal states, and slipped to others both human and animal? Perhaps they are some form of transubstantiation like the sacramentary of Catholic consecration. No one seems to know, any more than they know if God is out there behind the moon or inside it somewhere. There will always be enough room and real estate for slippers in the brains of the living, because the birth rate is much higher than the death rate, and the souls can't keep up.

These books are fictional autobiographies, and the narration reliably unreliable at times, though well flagged. They are written by a trinity that inhabits itself: Triple Suiter, Aubrey Shallcross, and Charles Porter.

The series is dedicated to the Hearing Voices Network, a worldwide organization that provides solace for voice hearers, both those in a very bad state and those who function well and have found a peace. The three of us above, are not committing theft from this community in telling these stories, we belong to the same hold.

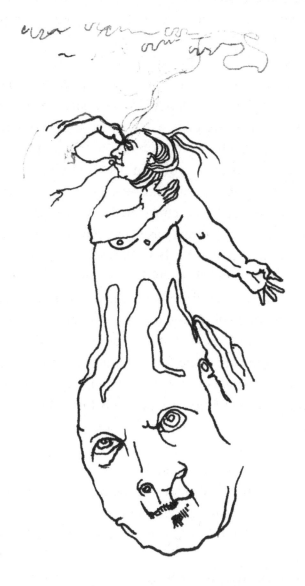

Preamble

I, Triple Suiter, a slipper, ride in the saloon of the psyche and stand in its eye. I have been known by many names throughout history and possess knowledge and *verstand* from other times, sliding blood to blood, brain to brain, as noumenon and then phenomenon you hear and sometimes see, but does not bleed. I live in the land of the subconscious; other than a deep dream state, the clearest view you have of that land is when I move into the conscious mind as the go-between, then I am wrongly called a figment of the imagination, a maggot, a dream, schizophrenia, and other invented terms. Aubrey Shallcross can hear and see me from the conscious side. I am not a product of his mind. I exist. I am, as much as you *are*.

The pure analogue part of Aubrey, the perception of himself as "I" and the single point of view, is gone because of me, yet he appears normal. He conceals how he is from people, but not from himself. In Africa, he would be considered divine; in the West, he would be called mental, kaleidoscopic – a psychotic talk-walker. The audible events and figurines of slippers have inhabited the spaces of humanity's conscious and subconscious for eons as our brains strained to change and evolve over time. True, there are two worlds, but they can't be explained by Plato – only schizophrenia.

You don't know much about Aubrey if you haven't read *Shallcross* and *Flame Vine*. They stand on their own, though they are closely related. This book, *Shallcross: Animal Slippers*, follows the other two. Charles Porter, Aubrey, and I, gave those books to Sonny's Book Store in Stuart, Florida, years ago. They tell the Tom Sawyer and Julian Jaynes truth. Some things are stretched, but mostly, they tell the truth.

PART ONE

Chapter 1: THE CONSECRATION

In 1974, a Black Seminole Indian, Billie Monday, sat on a creek in white man's clothes, clothes from a store in Ft. Pierce, Florida, called Ranchland. His shirt was snap-button and he wore a cowboy hat, creased and ventilated. You'd sense he was an Indian because he chanted and threw dust on a fire, like an Indian.

Lying beside him motionless, except for the eyelids that blinked on and off, were two monstrous alligators – *allapattas*, they were called in the Seminole language. One had two toes missing from its left front foot, the other had high scutes, or bony osteoderms down the middle of his tessellated back. Listening and chanting with the swamp water, crickets, pig frogs, and a highway, the Indian put a hand in the air and pointed to the sky; with a finger from his other, he drew a design on each gator's head in the colors of war paint.

Out of the dark came a younger man, and like Billie Monday, he was of mixed blood, Seminole and black. He sat with Billie, the old mossback *yaholi*, or medicine man. Billie put the same paint on the man he put on the gators, then handed him two cane knives with teeth attached to the bottom edge – long, pointed alligator teeth with turquoise imbedded in them like those of a vicious pimp.

During the first six months of that year, three people were killed by alligators, all white males, and when their mauled remains were found, each one's head was missing. There were other killings at the time by a human called the Tin Snip Killer, and these got as much attention. People love atrocity, each of us a loving beast. The last Tin Snip victim was a man who butchered veal

1

calves for a living. His body was found inside a standing refrigerator surrounded by cleaved cow parts, a note pinned to his shirt that read, "He offended nature." The man was holding a Polaroid picture of his dead self. Those killings stopped, but an alligator killed a man yesterday on the creek.

Chapter 2: DEATH OF THE RICHARDS TWINS

ANIMAL SLIPPERS

FEBRUARY, 1994

Yesterday on the creek, Shane Richards, now in his eighties, was getting himself straight. His old, frail dog lay next to him on the sofa. Plastic lines hooked to skin-buried needles in the dog's foreleg and Mr. Richards's left arm ran to a large syringe held by Mary Kincaid, a licensed veterinarian in the state of Florida; she was crying and bleeding from a bullet wound in her foot. A pamphlet, *Peace for Pets: We come to your home*, lay on the floor. Shane Richards lifted his right arm, pointed a pistol at her, and said, "You must put my dog and me down at the same time, after I tell you about my brother and confess his murder."

The woman nodded, held her throbbing foot, and Shane Richards began to curate a story. It would be half an hour before the story was over, the man and the dog were dead, and Ms. Kincaid would recall for police every word he told her.

"I killed my brother this morning. He was my identical twin. We are the get of a good family. Both of us graduated from Stetson University up in Deland and have degrees in English and minors in history. We left that world, came home, and ran our parents' fish camp. Somehow we were able to keep our love of the arts and manage the business. Eventually, we bought the place from our folks and renamed it Shy Brothers' Fish Camp.

"We were well known hunting and fishing guides. We read books at night, never owned a TV or subscribed to a newspaper, and never married. Had an attitude about, as my brother used to say, 'Getting stuck in the centripetal wet-hole-suck of the modern trivial self.' Proud antiques. That was us. Throw-backs and admirers of legendary Florida hunters like Glen Simmons and Totch

5

Brown over in Chokoloskee, men who lived in the lost world of the glade hammocks and mangroves, the 'shadow lands,' Peter Matthiessen called them.

"We are, were, identical twins – Shane and Lane, our mother named us. We were punch-outs of each other. Duple darlings. Our dad taught us about hard work. Dad used to hold up the baking soda boxes in the grocery store and point to the Arm and Hammer picture while we stood quiet. He said that picture meant work.

"A lot of gator hunting for hides went on back then. In our forties, we noticed this marked gator following us when we fire-hunted at night. He was a fourteen-foot bull with high scutes, those anatomicals that stick up along their backs, and his were so tall he looked dragonish when they stuck out of the water. The top of his nose had rises of serrated bone, almost as if they had been designed in some shipyard for a particular function. He was too big to kill for his hide because a hide is not marketable after a gator is over seven feet long. Too thick. A 'button hide' it's called, though I don't know the etymology of that word. Probably some grand argot or cryptonym from the old cracker people, God bless them. The gator never threatened us in those years, just followed us sometimes. My brother decided because of that high ridge on his back he would call him The Dragon, and we wouldn't kill him unless we had good reason."

"My foot is bleeding, Mr. Richards. I need a hospital," said Mary Kincaid, looking up from the floor.

"Okay. A little bit longer, and we'll get this done. I've been hurt a lot worse than you are right now. Hell, it's just a little 22-caliber bullet I put through there. Offer it up or something, would you? Now, where was I? Yes.

"A man we grew up with, a man who knew gators like us, waded into the water once with this Dragon monster back in the

50s. This was not uncommon among cracker boys when they got intoxicated with their friends and wanted to dance with a snake like a Pentecostal. Well, this man, Drayton Shallcross, said he just wanted to see what that gator's eye had in it because it seemed almost friendly. Ole Drayton was going to hook onto that eye and find out. He did have a 9mm pistol in his hand. That gator got as close as thirty feet to him, and then it was as if he looked right at his gun. He went under water again and disappeared. And guess what! Ms. Kincaid, are you listening?"

"Yes, Mr. Richards, but my foot is making me miserable. Can't we stop? We can say my foot was an accident. You were showing me your gun collection or…"

"No, no, no. I must finish my story before I finish myself. And I might finish you, girl, if you don't grit your teeth and cooperate."

"But…"

"Then!"

"But…"

"Then…! There was the time Drayton's son, Aubrey, stepped into the water with that gator when he was maybe fifteen. We all held our breaths and guns but didn't point them. Aubrey was talking to the thing, but he seemed to be talking to someone inside his own head, too. I heard the kid say something like, 'Do think he will come for me? Can you see the little man standing in his eye, like my dad told me? You can. Should I get closer?' After that, the gator went down. That kid said he saw Captain Nemo standing in its eye. Said it made the eye look like the big bubble window on Nemo's submarine, the *Nautilus*. That gator seemed drawn to Aubrey, as if it were part human. I said before there was something about that thing not dangerous, almost trustworthy. We really didn't want to shoot him. Aubrey said Nemo told it what to do. His father, Drayton, turned to my brother and said, 'Aubrey

7

always loved *20,000 Leagues under the Sea.* 'Course, we just nodded. You know that one, don't you, Ms. Kincaid?"

"Who is Captain Nemo, Mr. Richards?" she asked, her voice shaking.

"Oh, God help us, you science majors! You get such an education. You haven't heard of *20,000 Leagues under the Sea*? Hell, it's all about science."

"I have, but I don't remember the story."

"Have you read *Moby Dick*?"

"No."

"Take a look at those two after this is over if you can sit still that long. You've noticed that I have been referring to my brother and myself in the past tense because it *is* over." He took a breath.

Mary Kincaid looked around the room. A lamp stand made from a fat gator foot disappeared up into a shade above it with pictures of mermaids on it. Two large, bleached gator skulls sat on a sideboard. There were tabletop pictures of the two men standing with kill trophies – thick, long alligators hanging from cross arms under an oak tree, and another picture of them holding up a six-foot rattlesnake by the neck.

"And there was a second gator this size around, too, but mean," Shane Richards went on. "That one was dangerous. I had a close call with this saurian Grendel once. My brother and I were fire-hunting one night in a pole skiff when we saw a flashlight down through the woods along the creek. We didn't know that mean gator was right behind our skiff, stalking us. When we poled closer to the light and looked through the trees, this guy we knew to be a friend of Drayton's kid Aubrey was there. We got even closer, and of all things, we saw him putting a body inside an old refrigerator. He shoved the refrigerator, body and all, into a big hole in the ground then started to shovel dirt on top. It was dark as hell that night. We had seen the man once before, talking to Aubrey at a boat landing. Just then, that big gator came up on the bank behind us and reached for my leg, but he missed and tore off my shoe. We couldn't shoot. We didn't want the man burying the body to see us, and I think that gator knew it, so he took the chance. He was smart, like The Dragon gator, but malicious, as if something inside him talked to Faust or swamp devils. I don't know. Anyway, after he missed me, he slid back in the water, and that's when we saw he had only two toes on his left front foot. My brother said he'd heard of a giant gator up in the panhandle called Two-Toed Tom. There were all these stories about him killing mules, children, cattle, women. They organized hunts for him, but he just disappeared. They still have a festival up there called the Two-Toed Tom Festival. Amazing the prevarications people make up about killer gators and their urge to glorify them with parties, don't you think, Ms. Kincaid? But I'm not making this story of mine up, and, oh yeah, we never messed with the man burying the body, even though we thought he might be this fellow that owned a little store downtown. None of our business, you see. Backwoods business. You stay out of that.

"Now you sure you have thirty cc's of propofol in that horse syringe you've got there? Hold it up so I can see it."

She raised her hand. The black markings on the cylinder satisfied him.

"Yep, that's the quantity most states would use for execution. I researched it. Anyway, my brother was a Florida history scholar." He leaned back against the sofa, holding the gun on her. "And he was amazed that Two-Toed Tom, if that was really him, had made it all the way down here from North Florida, but gators have been known to go very long distances."

"Please, Mr. Richards, come to your senses. Where is this all going?"

"What do you mean, Doctor? It's going to the grave. That's where. I'm the one about to die here. You're just sitting on the floor with a small bullet hole in your footsy listening to good history from a dead man. No one knows the inside on this with my brother and me. Now I'm almost done with the story, so quit trying to keep me from getting this off my chest before I die." He coughed and looked at the gun in his hand. Turned it over flat and then upright again.

"An old Seminole medicine man we knew, Billie Monday, told my brother and me this. Osceola, the great warrior from the 1800s, was a fine, honorable human being just trying to protect his people and land. He was impossible to catch or beat in a fight, and frustrated, the army's General Jessup promised him a peace talk under a white flag. When Osceola came to talk, the general double crossed him and incarcerated him. There was an explosion in the press about the ethics of what Jessup had done, but that didn't stop people from stealing more Seminole land. You know the classic double standard regarding that history of ours and the Indians, and this thing with Osceola gets worse.

"In prison, Osceola, because of his fame and good looks – all tall, high bones in his face, large eyes – well, the artists of the day wanted to paint him in his plumed turban and silver belt with bone handle knife. He was of mixed race, you know. His father was white and his mother Creek, white, and African. He was a 'painted bird,' like that writer Jersey Kosinsky said in his book. Hybrid vigor was his. He was a great athlete, the best at Indian ball games, running, and wrestling. He was well spoken and fierce in battle. The artist George Catlin painted him shortly before he became sick and died of a sepsis in prison. And this is the weird part. His prison doctor, Dr. Weedon, a known eccentric, cut off Osceola's head after he died and hung it in his children's bedroom. I mean, *his* children's bedroom, Ms. Kinkaid, and he told his kids if they were bad, the head of the great savage would come back to life and get them. Excellent parenting, wouldn't you say, Doctor? A sacrilege of some smashed-up kind. God damn it, there is something like a hundred streets, three counties, lakes and places galore in Florida named after that warrior. And before those Florida State football games, some kid comes flying out to midfield on a spotted horse and plants a spear, and guess what they call him. The kid, I mean."

"Osceola," Mary Kincaid mumbled, staring at the floor she sat on, cradling her foot.

"Right. That man was worshipped by people on both sides of the Seminole War. He was the real thing. No stand-ins, stunt men, or other movie macaronis. He was as real as we are in this room right now, about to do what we are about to do, and there is nothing counter-factual about it for you or for me tonight."

"Please, Mr. Richards, this is murder, not suicide, if I do this to you. It is well known that when people reconsider killing themselves, they are glad they didn't when they look back."

"Dr. Kincaid, I murdered my twin brother this morning, and I shot you in the foot. I'm quite finished with my life, and the prospect of prison is untenable. I'm almost to my brother's murder. Be patient.

"There were incidents in this county and the next two counties back in the 70s. I mean alligator incidents. Three people were killed. Such things happen in Florida. Hell, the newspapers pay more attention to sharks and lightning down here than alligators, but gators kill more people, and a lot of people just disappear. The heads of these victims were bitten off, and an easier-to-eat arm or leg was gone, too, but gators usually don't bite off a head. Too bony and big. Authorities never found the heads, only the chewed-on bodies. You see, gators don't feed on something big out in the water. They won't swallow something out there 'cause they don't like to swallow water, so most of the time they take their kills to the bank. Cops found small pieces of Seminole cloth on the bank near the bodies – those colored, fortress-looking patterns the Indians wear, you know, but no one knew where they came from. Spooky, ain't it? The Indians and ranchers rumored that this gator, Two-Toed Tom, did the killing and took the heads, and hid them in his secret den. Lane, my brother, said the Indians claim the great warrior Osceola lives inside that gator, come back as a spirit to get revenge because he needs his head to enter the City of the Dead. Indians think his spirit wanders, looking for it, and has taken up residence in that animal to cover ground and find it. My brother thought Osceola was controlling that gator, like Aubrey said Captain Nemo controlled The Dragon. Lane said Osceola's ghost killed and took the heads of white men because they took his, and that the Seminole cloth was left every time so people would know."

Mary Kincaid looked at him now, and Shane Richards saw some small interest in her pained face.

"My brother was the stronger one, though we grew together in the womb and shared the same blood and spit. He was different from me when it came to assertions and dares. Sometimes he made me feel like a male dog that squats to piss instead of lifting a leg, if you will excuse me for saying that. He could, my brother, whip his weight in wildcats, and he read everything from Zane Grey to Greek tragedy. He was also preoccupied by the story of Gilgamesh from 7th century BC, and said he and I were each other's alter egos and trusted friends, like Gilgamesh and Enkidu, Achilles and Patroclus, David and Jonathan. My brother's favorite modern novella was *Legends of the Fall*, by a man named Jim Harrison. Have you read it, Dr. Kincaid?"

She shook her head.

"At the end of the book, the aging main character confronts a large grizzly bear, and they lock up in battle. Readers never know, but one can imagine the four hundred-pound grizzly won, and so did the man in a way, by dying like a real man and warrior. And that's the way my brother saw himself – a warrior, like Osceola, and he told me that was the way he would like to die, instead of from some pale sickness."

Shane Richards got quiet and reached over to a side table for some water with the arm that had the needle in its crook.

"Then it happened, Ms. Kincaid. My brother had a stroke. We are in our eighties, you know. Who said, 'Nothing spoils like the future'? Was that Henry James or ole Fitzy Fitzgerald? Anyway, after a year's time, he said he wasn't going to live like this anymore. There were always gators hanging out on our creek, hoping to get scraps from the fishing parties we booked. Did you know alligators can live to be ninety, maybe a hundred years old? I mean, they've been around two million years or something, but hell, their brain, they say, only weighs nine grams when they're full grown. Heard it will fit in a teaspoon.

"And so, my brother asked me to carry him down by the water in the mornings and put him in a lawn chair so he could look at the creek. He always had me bring him four pieces of toast with his coffee. He liked to watch the turtles and birds, he said. One morning, I saw him throwing toast on the water, chumming for gator, making those guttural sounds in his throat we make to get their attention when we hunt. I asked him what he was doing that for, and he told me that was how he wanted to die, just like the man in *Legends of the Fall* – locked in a death grip with a gator. You know, Ms. Kincaid, I understood, because my brother was so sick and infirm from his stroke. So, when he asked me to help him consummate his plan, I agreed.

"I thought about everything for a week, and then I made the appointment with you. And even though I told my brother once I'd rather die by snakebite or lightning than a gator, I quailed on that, too, and chose this needle in my arm." His leg started to shake. He took another drink of water. It went down the wrong way, and he had a coughing fit.

"Sorry. Old man stuff. Can't swallow reliably every time anymore. Back to my brother's resolution." He cleared his throat twice. "So, to do my part, I sat him out in his chair this morning like always, with his favorite hunting knife in his good hand and walked back to the house crying. Minutes later, through the kitchen window, I watched Two-Toed Tom himself, who I had not seen around here in the mornings, come out of the water, seize my brother by the legs, then lift him by the middle of his body and start towards the creek, the huge black thing walking way up high on its fat legs with Lane flopping in his mouth like a damn towel. The whole time, my brother never made a sound. Blood and urine squirting from his body and him stabbing that gator's buttoned hide with the knife bending and bouncing off that black armor; me crying, standing in the kitchen watching, crying louder and whispering, 'Arm and Hammer, Arm and Hammer,' until I was screaming it. The two of them went down in that water out there. My brother and I never killed an Indian, but we must've killed a thousand gators in our day, and Tom was getting even. I walked out and stood on the bank for a while and all I saw were bubbles coming up. My brother was right. There's something lives inside that thing that makes it evil as a goddamn Minotaur, and it just might be what's left of Osceola.

"And now you. You hand me that syringe you're holding. That way you can tell them you didn't actually put me and my old dog Lion here down. I did. I'm broken and tired of this life, and so is my dog, which will be no life for either one of us without my brother and our health."

Mary Kincaid did as she was told, the gun pointing at her in Shane Richards's other hand. He smiled at her, looked at a picture of himself and his brother hanging on the living room wall and said, "You tell the cops those two gators are still out there, and they're not normal. Those things are something turned real out of a story, some of it a bad story. That Two-Toed creature is larcenous, but I don't think The Dragon one is. Goodnight, Ms. Kincaid. Goodnight, infinity."

He pushed the plunger in slow increments at first, then a big one. Just before his head fell over, he said, "Maybe if it was Captain Nemo or God that Shallcross boy was talking to in the water with the gator that day, that's where I'm headed. I... I think, I..."

An hour later, the police found Shane Richards and his dog on the sofa, their dead mouths open, plastic tubes and needles still in place. The next morning, divers found the mauled body of Lane Richards on the creek bottom. Mr. Richards's head and one arm were gone. The coroner nodded and said, "Yep. Gator did this," as Two-Toed Tom moved his big tail back and forth to slide him along another creek three miles away. He tucked the head of Lane Richards up under a high shelf to rot with three other heads, long turned to skulls, heads he had taken off years ago.

ANIMAL SLIPPERS

Chapter 3: THE ANIMAL SLIPPERS

Once a month, Aubrey Shallcross took a horse to a spot along the creek and camped to be alone. He liked the backwoods air that kicked around what he had left of the cowboy in him. In his sleeping bag at five-thirty in the morning, his brain was at a station called the Hypnopomic, the half-dream, half-woke place. His eyes were closed, but the lids went clear like a miracle. He saw two large alligators, an armadillo, and a coach whip snake around his campfire. Each animal had a Jiminy Cricket-sized person beside it called a slipper – homunculus forms, three to four inches tall, from the world of mental cases and mystics, a sort of unreliable experience to most, seemingly a dream.

One of the slippers claimed to be Captain Nemo from *20,000 Leagues under the Sea*. Nemo stood on the nose of his alligator and gave a speech about the environment. Another introduced himself as the famous Seminole Osceola, and he gave a speech about racism and betrayal. With the armadillo and the coach whip snake was a slipper named Martha, a Gypsy woman. She said her armadillo could start a fire by snapping its toenails together, and her snake could pick any lock on earth with its prehensile tongue. The group had dual causes – to intercede against poisonous land use and to disrupt housing developments with toxic trails. Martha said she would like to help.

In the gray, Aubrey saw his own slipper, Triple Suiter, leave him, go down his arm, and talk to the others in the circle. When

Aubrey came out of the dream they were gone. It was just him, his tied-out horse, and a morning cloud that broke off the moon.

Chapter 4: THE NOT-SO-ONLY CHILD

I've been thinking about Aubrey, me, Charles Porter – the hold of his history – the stratigraphy of his life. How years ago, *2001: A Space Odyssey* had a huge effect on his free dance – that rising monolith, those apes, the music, the jawbone weapon.

In the beginning for all of us, there was no jawbone, no carnival, no books, no film, no roads, just tracks on the ground – mastodon, ape, cow, human. Later came paths, ruts, piled rocks, blacktops, interstates, tire tracks, soundtracks, contrails, bronze plaques, and destroyed guard rails next to station after station of roadkill cross. That's what Aubrey Shallcross saw in his seen dreams, those crosses that say someone's name and "Drive Safely" at the top, instead of "Jesus, King of the Jews." He saw them when his friend died from a snake bite, when another was crushed by a machine, and as an altar boy when he carried the Solar Monstrance for the priest through clouds of incense. He saw them when Bette Middler's song, "The Rose," came through the radio of his truck and he hit a light pole.

And I've been thinking about Aubrey's other voice, Triple Suiter – the talks they've had – Aubrey's strange house, the taxidermy and mannequins in his living room, his views and opinions of people, and his fascination with the bumper sticker, *"JESUS PAID FOR OUR SINS, NOW LET'S GET OUR MONEY'S WORTH."*

I think about the irony of his last name: Shallcross – his interest in crossroads, cruciforms, four-way stop signs, and his constant struggle to leave Catholicism for some other state of grace. I think about his comatose visions after the man called Carlos shot him and he found himself talking to people on Roman kill trees out in the wetlands, before he went under the wing of a spoonbill to dream.

It's been two years since Carlos put a bullet in Aubrey's head. Carlos, who came to kidnap and rape Aubrey's love, Christaine. Then chaos and that bullet. For a moment, Aubrey thought he was in a movie, thought it was the dreaded "country visit" from *A Clockwork Orange* or *In Cold Blood*. Seconds later, Christaine and her father killed Carlos. Now everyone is trying to heal. A metal plate covers the hole in Aubrey's skull; his hair has grown back. He and Christaine have a five-year-old son named Drayton.

For Aubrey, there is too much free time, and he feels something has been rearranged in his brain, maybe from that bullet. He still schools his horses in the mornings and trains with Christaine's father, the riding master. In the afternoon, capillary thought takes him to a big room, a capacious cyclorama in his mind with a version of the Eiffel Tower in the middle of a cane field. Around the tower he flies, permuting things into a proto-corpus that pleases him, pushing on the elan of objects, music, books, film, and thoughts from his storied life, especially when that part of his brain he calls the "Mess Hall" comes and he is molested by agnosticism and existential cramps.

I remember when his mind split, after his father was dragged off a tractor by a flame vine – killed. The bohemia of his life in that wilderness after, the wildness of his twenties and thirties, the band he was in and Leda, his young wife – their happiness, their cross threads, her drugs, their end.

I think about The Blue Goose, a bar based on the short-sleeve shirt. The friends went there to laugh and sing around a table in the 70s, doing their "Oh, yeahs" from the movie *Seven Beauties*. So much happiness in those times until Leda left him, his friend The Junior died, and the other things that happened after that generation of star flies, bar flies, and Super Fly began to age. Now he only has one friend from the old group, John Chrome, and at age fifty, after all that has happened, two beatitudes remain – Christaine and his boy Drayton.

ANIMAL SLIPPERS

Chapter 5: THE STORY AT NIGHT

To Aubrey, his five-year-old son was something biblical with background music. He wanted all his attention. It was hard to get him to go to sleep so he made up a fascinator, a serial bedtime story that went on and on about two alligators and their animal friends, based on tales he was told as a boy and his recent early-morning dream about the animals on the creek around his campfire.

Aubrey worked the tale. Didn't know where it would go. He had grown up in the Florida world of backwoods and beaches and was sure he was his own best material. He liked props. A taxidermist friend put an eight-foot alligator in Drayton's bedroom so the boy could pretend to ride it and make noises while Aubrey told the stories to him.

Because his mind is the way it is, Aubrey lives with three points of view: those of the slipper Triple Suiter, his own thoughts, and a confusing name from somewhere – Charles Porter. The story he tells his son wanders through those minds like a *Ouija* finger and comes out fine for a child.

"This is the tale of two alligators," he always began. "The Seminoles call the alligators *allapattas*. One alligator had big, tall fins on his back and was called the Dragon, the other had only two toes on one front foot, and his name was Two-Toed Tom. They were protected by their guardian angels, or what Daddy calls a slipper, just as your guardian angel and slipper protects you.

"Once upon a time ....
....
....alligator.
   " ....
....
....carburet.

"...
.................................mansion.
"...
....
....
....
....
...................................red means run, son.
"..
....
....
....
...................righty tighty, lefty loose.
"..
....
....Turn   the
page. Sleep now. Slip away, Drayton."

Chapter 6: THE BLACK SEMINOLE,
FREDDIE TOMMIE

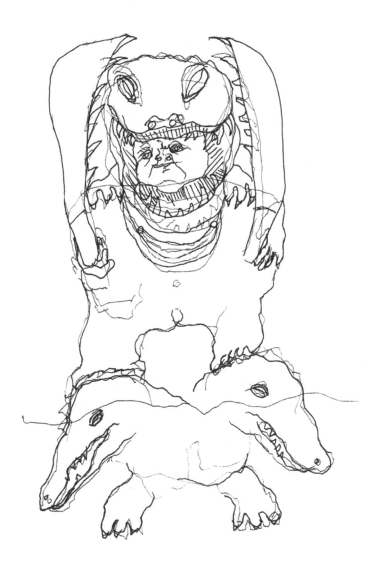

The young Indian who was given the cane knives by the medicine man years ago was a veteran of the war in Asia, and had come back to the reservation he grew up on. He tried to live in places other than Indian land, but he was part black, descended from runaway slaves who lived and fought with the Seminoles in the old wars. Because of the way he looked, he had to endure the "crowbar" – the Jim Crowbar. It was nigger this and nigger that, in an intransigent Bible Belt Florida of the 1970s; anyone dark was a nigger to those kinds of white people.

His full name was Freddie Cowkeeper Tommie; his father Seminole and black, his mother Seminole, white, and Spanish. He was handsome, tall, a good athlete, and after what the war did to him, the human version of the famous, terrible, and sublime. He had to do repulsive things in Vietnam, and that, like all of us, was what he was capable of as an animal and a man from each of the races he inherited. When Freddie returned in '71, he had one friend in town who had fought with him in the war, a white man called The Junior, Aubrey Shallcross's best friend.

Freddie soon got crazy. Wandered into a pixilated state of mind, became incapable of laughter and no longer understood joking. The tribe's medicine man, Billie Monday, was, in a way of walking, Freddie's minister. He occupied Freddie's mind with tribal medicine and obligation to help him slake his broken life. For Billie Monday, Freddie would do anything. He killed certain white men in the 70s, at Billie's request, with the sacred tooth-studded cane knives Billie gave him. He killed them in honor of Osceola, betrayed by the whites, his head taken so his soul could not enter the City of the Dead. The tooth marks from the blades Freddie used convinced authorities that the kills were gator kills. He always left a small piece of Seminole cloth at the scenes. The law didn't know what to make of that, but the Indians did. They knew it was the work of their *yaholi*, Billie Monday, the human *allapatta*. Two more deaths around that time came from the real gator, Two-Toed Tom, who the Indians believed carried the transubstantiated soul of the great Osceola in his eyes.

Freddie had come home a decorated vet, but you wouldn't see him with a bumper sticker or bill hat that said so, and you'd never see him at a VFW. He worked first in the Seminole Smoke Shop, selling tax free cigarettes, and then in the bingo halls on the reservation in Dania, next to Ft. Lauderdale, where the table gambling and property empire had not yet come around for the tribe. One day, though, the Seminoles would do something as big as stalemating the Indian war with the United States a hundred years ago; they would be the first tribe to win Class III gambling rights in a high court, the right to have casino table gambling on their land, not just the cheaper take from smoke shops and bingo. That got the tribe the revenue needed for self-governance and the funds to preserve its culture, and ironically, offered the white man a small recompense for diseases, murder, and misery, by giving the white man back *his* disease – gambling and drinking. After the Supreme Court ruled in their favor, other tribes built casinos and owed the Seminoles forever.

The *yaholi* taught Freddie to hate invasive species – any plant or animal that showed up in the biota like the white man had with his massacres and measles. The *yaholi* especially hated the Brazilian pepper tree, brought to Florida by the whites for its ornamental appearance in 1898. Here the plant became a hybrid, tough and cancerous to native species, hardier than the original plant in Brazil. It grew out of control, covering 3,000 square km of land, destroying edible plants that were food for native fauna. The birds spread the red seeds, and Florida was helpless, spending millions to control it; if they chopped it down, burned it, or ploughed it under, it's legacy powers brought it back in the same place. The largest uproar came from the Seminoles when it choked off food for the white tail deer in the Florida Panther National Park. Deer had sustained the sacred panthers. Most of the panthers were gone, but Indians believed their spirits still walked the palmettoes and sloughs at night.

Billy Monday had noticed something. He knew when the sand hill cranes ate the berries of native myrtles something happened in the birds' guts, and whatever it was made their droppings lethal to the peppers. The *yaholi* kept this secret from everyone except Freddie, his disciple. All it took was one bird pellet to send a toxin into the ground during wet season, some allelopathic effect in the dirt's microbial rhizome that created a knockdown effect on the peppers and erased their legacy powers and comeback ability.

Freddie went to stand after stand of wax myrtles after their berries came in and followed the sand hill cranes as they ate, leaving plenty of droppings for Freddie and the botanical potion needed to kill peppers. He did this alone and camped for days in different areas. When the summer rains came, the tree ground he had touched made the trees die. It made Freddie somewhat of a magic man among the Indians, an unknown magic science would love to know about.

He had a day job with a local white, Claddy Nelson, the cousin of his old army friend, The Junior Nelson. Claddy had a land clearing and tractor service, but not even Claddy, a drinker and older hell raiser, knew how Freddie did what he did to the peppers and didn't seem to care.

In 1985, a problem surfaced on the reservation in Broward County. A certain cocky and disliked deputy sheriff caused trouble with the tribe. He bragged about having a law degree and kept the University of Florida alumni license plate on his car very clean. His coffee cup said LITIGATOR on the side, another headline that turned off his coworkers. The deputy subtracted revenue from the tax-free cigarettes sold on Seminole land by stopping trucks carrying tobacco products into the smoke shops. He harassed the drivers with trumped up traffic violations, and tribal leaders had to pay him off to lay him off. Certain tobacco distributors did not want to sell to the tribe anymore. The graft was unknown to the sheriff, and when he was told, he shook his head and said, "Impossible. Not one of my men."

The tribe's chief went to the *yaholi*, Billie Monday. Billie said he would put a spell on the deputy using a splinter from a pine tree hit by lightning. Instead, he told Freddie to do what he was taught to do with the cane knives.

The deputy, an avid snook fisherman, went often to a mangrove area on the New River in Broward. He would cut his motor, bending low as he poled through channels towards the recesses of wet grottos, looking for the single-striped game fish. Freddie followed him, waiting.

Out of the water in the shallows one night, a tall, hard-shelled pupa rose and cracked out of its chrysalis of mud and river grass in the shape of a man. It had a large alligator skull with open mouth for its head, and inside the open mouth was a face, Freddie's face, war painted. Huge, amputated gator feet sat on each of Freddie's shoulders, and Freddie's muscled chest was bare except for a half-moon piece of silver he wore, said to have belonged to Osceola.

The deputy was frozen – seen-a-perfect-monster-frozen – unable to make something real out of it. Freddie smiled, stretched his arms out in front of him, and made the open and closed jaw movements University of Florida football fans make with those arms, then with one hand on the rail of the skiff, the other coming fast, he whacked the deputy's neck with a tooth studded cane knife and grabbed him by the shirt, pulling him out of the boat before the spurting blood could stain the floor boards. It had to look like a gator kill. Gators wouldn't come into a boat. The man kicked in the water of the creek while Freddie held him under so his lungs would fill. The coroner would say an alligator did this. Gators drown things first.

When the man was dead, Freddie hacked off his head with the knives, leaving teeth marks on the neck stump. He cut off an arm. He made more teeth marks on the torso and legs, evidence for the coroner. Last, Freddie took the body to the bank and dropped a small piece of Seminole cloth so the tribe would know it was the work of Billie Monday. The deputy's head was bagged with the severed arm and taken to the medicine man for praise and approval, where it was placed on a cypress stump altar by the creek and spoken to. Billie Monday then gave the head to Two-Toed Tom, who brought it to his hideout the next day and put it with the other heads up under the creek bank cave he had hollowed out years ago.

The second time Freddie killed, the *yaholi* prepared him as usual with a ceremony on the creek. Freddie sat in the dark by a fire and chanted with Billie Monday until the Dragon and Two-Toed Tom walked their fourteen-foot bodies out of the water and laid down beside them. A poacher had been coming into the Brighton reservation, taking gators and game. The hunter was also known to go out around the Harris Ranch that bordered the creek where Tom and the Dragon sometimes hid, and where Aubrey Shallcross camped with his horse. Freddie followed the trespassing man for a week. When he was sure he would hunt one night, he went to the

31

creek with the *yaholi* and they summoned the two big gators.

Around a fire, wearing sand hill crane wings on the back of his arms, Billie Monday put war paint on Freddie, Tom, and the Dragon. The slippers, Nemo and Osceola, stood in their gators' eyes at attention respectfully, their hands behind their backs, battle looks on their faces. When the ceremony was over, the gators went to the water and lined up side by side so Freddie could stand on their backs, one foot on each, a Roman rider of the never-before-seen, created from the world we don't know, moving down the creek towards a spot a half mile away. There, the poacher would pass, looking for the red eyes of *allapattas* to kill for hides.

Freddie stood on the swimming monsters, proud and amazed, living what the white man would scoff at as a drunken Indian tale. White men, making their happy-hunting-ground-rain-dance jokes when they could in Vietnam and Florida bars, but Freddie knew at least one white man tonight who would see something he never thought he'd see before he went to his tomb. It would almost be worth letting him go, so he could tell his white friends and be laughed at like the whites laughed at Indians when they spoke of their chimerical visions. But no, he would not. It was this white man's night.

"Death from the water," Freddie said out loud to the creek. "Death from the swamp. Death from the nigger Indian," he said even louder and laughed for once.

Things began happening behind him as he moved further down the waterway. Congeries of other gators came from the mangroves and back part swamps, swimming with Freddie and the monsters. A strange flotilla formed, resemblant of people coming out of buildings and side streets to fall in for a street fight.

After some time, Freddie saw the poacher in the dark. He came in closer. The man heard guttural sounds from a throat and thought it was a gator, but the sound came from Freddie's throat. The Dragon went under and came up on the other side of the man's boat, waiting to bump it if the man pulled his gun.

The poacher pointed his headlight out on the creek and felt his flesh crack from what he saw – gators galore, red eyes by the hundreds. A certain agnostic disbelief set in. He rubbed his eyes. Couldn't tell what he was looking at and was afraid. He heard the guttural sounds again, turned and saw his imprecator, Freddie, sanctified in gator parts, war paint, and Seminole dress. The poacher's lips smacked. A radiolarian choir welled up with a Church of Jesus organ, the same choir the man's family heard when they baptized him as a baby. In a makeshift move, Freddie pulled him from the boat into the morcellating mouth of Two-Toed Tom, the poacher's own mouth so open Freddie saw the top part of his heart beating in the back. Two-Toed sank him for the drowning part and spun his big tail to drive the death roll. Freddie went into a stare like he used to in Vietnam, his eyes working nothing, as the choir went to a high part and the water blew bed sheet clouds of blood.

Tom came up with the body and swam to the bank. He took off an arm, chewed briefly, and swallowed it whole, throwing his head back in jerks to get it down. Chunks and other gobbets where taken out of the thighs and buttocks until the gator had enough and rested. Freddie swam to the bank and sat with Tom and the mauled body. The Dragon stayed close by in the water. Inside the eyes, Captain Nemo and a satisfied Osceola stood nodding to each other. Freddie had been told by the *yaholi* that in this case, Tom would be the one to kill and bite off the man's head. No cane knives. He said Tom would carry the head back to the place where they started, the same place Aubrey camped when the animal slippers came out of the creatures in his fireside dream. Freddie dropped the small piece of Seminole cloth on the bank.

The flotilla streamed back to the *yaholi*, Billie Monday, the Seminole warrior standing on the two bulls. Two-Toed Tom held the poacher's head in his mouth, the man's eyes wide open in their last moment, and the mouth was wrong, crooked, its lower jaw broken. Osceola and Nemo's small forms stood on the long noses of their vessels like captains of German U-boats returning home in the Baltic.

The Seminole chief found them the next day and kneeled in front of the *yaholi* to give his thanks. All of this happened years before the Richards twins died, and before Aubrey Shallcross did his part in this preternatural story of pursuit, repose, pursuit, death, and repose, to fight for what they all considered mansion and just.

Chapter 7: THE DRAGON AND TWO-TOED TOM

ALLAPATTA MACHINA

"This is the tale of two alligators. Get in bed, my darling young one. Be still and listen, child. The Indians call alligators *allapattas*. On a summer day, a mommy *allapatta* felt full in her belly. At a place on the creek, she made a mound by pushing sticks and grass into a pile. She laid forty-five white eggs that looked like the chicken eggs Mommy cooks you for breakfast. She pushed sticks and mud over the eggs so the heat of the sun would warm them and they could hatch like you hatched. If it was a hot, hot summer, the sun would make all the babies into little boy gators. If the summer was cooler, they would be all little girl gators. If the heat was just a little hot, but not too hot, there would be both little gator boys and little gator girls.

The noise one day from the mound told the mommy to uncover it. First to crawl off the nest, pushing others out of the way with his nose, was a boy gator that would grow up to be called The Dragon, and the tiny gator's wish to lead with that nose would become mansion in the State of Florida, but now he would stay close to his mother until he was a little older, and a slipper (or guardian angel) named Captain Nemo found him to guide him through his life."

"What's mansoon, Daddy?"

"Oh. That word was 'mansion.' It means a big house. Daddy and his friend Mr. Chrome use that word to refer to anything that is a big deal or gets a lot of attention, and The Dragon is going to get plenty of that. You remember Mr. Chrome the schoolteacher, don't you?"

"Yes, sir."

"When the baby gator grew to be three feet long, he fought with a dog trying to steal a meal from him. Captain Nemo, who was living with the dog at the time, decided to leave the dog. He went through the gator's nose to set up house and be with the gator, so he could see what it would be like to be underwater again. He decided to stay and watch out for the Dragon for the rest of his life. This story is about the adventures they had.

"Once, Captain Nemo was not a slipper. He was a human being, like Daddy and you. A long time ago, he wrote books, and his name was Mr. Jules Verne. Mr. Vern was from the Loire River Valley in faraway France. In that beautiful place he wrote one of Daddy's favorite books, *20,000 Leagues under the Sea*."

"Was that a manshun, Daddy?"

"Yes. Yes, that book, it was a mansion. A big deal. Now you go to sleep, slip away, and tomorrow night I'll tell you about the other gator they call Two-Toed Tom. Turn the page."

"But there is no page, Daddy. You just tell me the story."

"I know. I just like the way it sounds to say that. Finished."

Chapter 8: THE DEPUTY

After he schooled the horse, Aubrey stepped off the big chestnut and handed the reins to Asante Sadacca's working student. Asante was his longtime riding coach in the sport of dressage. Asante, you could say, was also his common-law father-in-law, since Aubrey and Christaine were not married. At the first stop light after the farm, he thought about how he rode today and what he was doing riding again with a metal plate in his head; his neurosurgeon would drop him if he found out he was back on horses. He watched the red light. When it dropped to the yellow on the adjacent side, he put his foot on the brake and pushed the engine idle up. Bam! The light went to green and he popped the truck out, tires squealing, just to feel the bump like he was twenty again. Maybe he should be tuning cars instead of horses. It's safer for the brain injured. The business world, arm and hammer, that's where he was when he owned Shallcross Chrysler years ago, before he sold the company. Now with all this free time, the horses were magic, creatures he had grown up with – living, loving, interesting; not cold like a car – no blood, no heart, still. Very cool to do up a fast car, but he was more about blood and heart lately.

It was noon. He never ate lunch at home. Trip told him that old saw years ago about love: "For better or worse and lunch, don't get it," so he went to Jensen Beach, to The Blue Goose on the Indian River and ordered cracked conch, a salad, and ice tea while he reviewed the photos and taxidermy on the walls of the old place. When the food came, he opened his never-without magazine; something about eating and reading at the same time that worked. Maybe it was the serotonin food made in the brain that made a magazine read that much better. He even loved the word "magazine." So compact and organized, loaded with essay and bullets.

On his left arm stood the little man, Triple Suiter, his lifelong concierge and counselor. On his other arm was his tattoo, **SERENOA REPENS**, the binomial name for the scrub palmetto that surrounded his Florida town. Aubrey saw Trip looking at the walls of The Blue Goose, too. The sound system played a new song just out, with a line in the chorus: "What if God was one of us? Just a slob like one of us?"

His friend John Chrome, the brainy schoolteacher, walked in and sat. Triple Suiter went up Aubrey's arm and disappeared into his armpit.

"Schoolteacher. How you doin?"

"Exceptional. Wanna talk about some left pearls or that song that's on right now?" Chrome looked up at the black speakers in the bar.

"Yep, always wondered about that."

"What? God, a slob?"

"I'd go lookin for him again if I thought he was. I'd be talking to three on-the-tree, like I used to with the priesty boys."

"After you croak, I see it. You being guided by a psychopomps to heaven to meet the great Slob."

"What the fuck's a pyschopomps?"

"Roman god stuff. Want to surf? I hear it's four-foot out there."

"Not today, Chrome. I'm looking at some horses with Asante this afternoon."

"See the news? Those weird brothers that own the fish camp, one of them was killed by an alligator, and the other was put to sleep by a dog vet right there in his house. Talk about left pearls. I couldn't write that stuff."

"In today's paper?"

Chrome handed it to him.

"Shit. I knew those brothers forever. They were friends of my dad and The Junior's dad. A veterinarian, imagine that. Says here Shane Richards shot the vet in the foot to convince her he was serious."

"That would do it for me."

"Also says his brother Lane was taken right out of a lawn chair by a big gator."

Aubrey got home around six. There was a sheriff's car. A detective was sitting on the front porch with Christaine. Five-year-old Drayton was running around the yard, stopping occasionally to stare at the deputy and the gun he wore.

"This is Detective Kimmel, Aubrey," said Christaine. "I told him you'd be home and he said he'd like to wait."

Kimmel stood up and nodded. "Just like to ask you some questions about an incident, if I could, Mr. Shallcross. Your name was mentioned."

"This isn't about the Carlos thing a couple of years ago, is it?"

"No, sir. This is something that happened out at the Shy Brothers' Fish Camp on the South Fork yesterday."

"I just read about it."

"I understand you knew them."

"All my life. Friends of my father's, too."

"Yes, your father's name was mentioned."

"In what context?"

"Well, according to the woman at the scene – Dr. Mary Kincaid – Shane Richards told her you know the alligator that killed his brother Lane. Mr. Richards died by a chemical injection at the scene after his brother was killed, but he told Dr. Kincaid everything that happened with his brother and the gator, because he witnessed it. He gave her a long history of the events before his brother's death, and yours and your father's names came up. I know your father is deceased, so I'd like to ask what you know about the story."

"I don't know you. I know most of the deputies in my area."

"I've been here about three years, working in homicide. I've heard about you, though, and your unusual house. Is it still just sitting up there in the woods?"

"Yes. After what happened two years ago, we moved down to this end of the property. I rent the guest cottage up there to an old schoolmate, and she uses it in the daytime for a studio."

"Do you mind if I get her name? We like to know where everyone is in the area in case of emergencies."

"It's Nell Kitching. She just recently moved back here."

"I understand. Mr. Shallcross, is there a friend you thought capable of, or suspected of being involved in murder some years ago?"

"What? What murder? I mean, I'm friends with some cowboys in the west county I wouldn't want to cross."

"No, this is from fifteen or twenty years ago. Shane Richards told Dr. Kincaid he and his brother saw a man bury a body in a refrigerator one night when they were hunting, and he said the man was a friend of yours."

"What was his name?"

"Kincaid said Richards didn't give a name."

"A refrigerator? That sounds like the Tin Snip Killer, thirty years ago, a series of murders."

"Yes, it's a cold case I'm very interested in, and you're right about the timeline. Maybe Ms. Kincaid misunderstood that. Your friend who rents from you – is that the same Kitching family that lost a relative in those murders?"

"It is, but I don't know anyone I'd suspect of being that freak."

"Have you ever heard of two alligators people refer to as Two-Toed Tom and the Dragon?"

Aubrey chewed the inside of his cheek. "Sure. They killed some people years ago. The Richards brothers gave them those nicknames."

"We found tracks on the creek bank where the gator that killed Lane Richards came out of the water and went back in, and there were two toes missing on the left front foot. Shane said something about you wading in the water with one of those gators when you were a boy."

"I did. I was fifteen. It was The Dragon, but I can't believe that gator is still alive. They do seem to live forever, don't they? I never heard anything about The Dragon bothering anybody."

"Richards verified that Two-Toed Tom killed his brother. He saw it happen, and he was the one that put Lane out there in the chair by the water. Seems his brother knew that gator was there that day and actually chummed it in with some bread. Death by alligator. What you think of that?"

Aubrey chewed the inside of his cheek some more. Thought for a minute. "Like I said, I knew them. I know how they saw the world and their place in it. But you know, Mr. Kimmel, I've never seen that Tom gator, even when I used to hunt gators with my friends."

"We also found a small piece of Seminole cloth on the bank the next day where we think Mr. Richards was taken into the water."

"I bet if you check the records in the 70s, you'll find that cloth was found at the scenes of those other killings, too."

"I did, and it was. Now what do you think all that twilight stuff is about?"

"Don't know. The cloth? A prank? Don't know. What else did

he tell Ms. Kincaid? It didn't say in the paper today it was Two-Toed Tom."

"No. We kept his name out of the paper for a reason. Anyway, the story she heard was more twilight stuff, that Two-Toed Tom was possessed by an Indian out to get people because of what happened during the Indian wars. He also told her about finding the cloth in the past."

Aubrey stared at the deputy, who stared back at him.

Finally, the deputy scratched his cheek and sighed. "Here's my card. Call me if you remember anything about the person seen burying the body in the refrigerator." He stepped off the porch and turned around. "Shane told Ms. Kincaid the refrigerator man owned a store in downtown, in Stuart, if that helps." He left.

"Want a drink?" Christaine asked.

"Guess I do. Jesus Streptococcus Christ, what a sick story. That gator kill, and that other brother getting a vet to snuff him like that."

"About these brothers?"

"Yeah. I did walk into the water once with The Dragon. Now I'm upstairs spinning this tale to our son that I've taken from my past, and some of it seems to be coming true again." He showed her the newspaper John Chrome gave him at lunch.

"Tell me about these men and the time you spent around them."

"They were private. Smart. When I was a kid they said to me, 'Aubrey, son, you make sure you get a college education; once you have that, it's arm and hammer, arm and hammer, boy. You have to work hard. Outwork anybody you think is smarter than you.' From then on, I would see them or go over there with my father, and one of them always winked at me when we were leaving and said, 'Arm and hammer, Aubrey. Arm and hammer,' then held up a baking soda box from the kitchen. To this day, when I see baking soda, I think about those guys. The man burying the body in a refrigerator reminds me of the Tin Snip Killer. Richards said I knew the man, but I have no idea who it might be."

He told Christaine about the murders, but Christaine already knew some of the stories and that Nell Kitching's mother was one of the victims. She and Nell had talked about it once while Christaine held her hand and Nell cried, although she told Christaine she thought her mother had a can of meanness in her. She was only nine when her mother was murdered, and she wondered what their relationship would have been like if she had lived.

Aubrey said, "At those murder scenes, it was the Polaroid picture of the bodies holding a picture of themselves holding a picture of themselves holding a picture of themselves, inside those old white Frigidaires that fascinated and scared me. The picture on the Quaker Oat box thing, you know? It was the perfect example of infinite regression   the picture of the Quaker on the box, holding a picture of himself holding a picture of himself holding a picture of himself on the box, getting smaller and smaller. I used to think that's what happened to us when we die. We just get smaller and smaller like the Quaker until we disappear. Some terrifying image of self-erasure I carried around back then."

He told her more about The Dragon and the colored origins surrounding the existence of the other gator, Two-Toed Tom, considered the reincarnation of Osceola, who was getting even with the white man for keeping his soul in two parts by cutting off his head. He saw she liked the story. She was a staff writer for the *Miami Herald* when he met her seven years ago, and she had left the paper to be with him. She still wrote stories. He double-dog more than loved her. "Bow-legged blind" he loved her, he told someone once. It started before he ever met her and heard her name. Christaine. Did her parents name her that intentionally? Did they put those two words together, Christ and stain, like stain of

Christ? Blood stain of Christ? So Catholic it was from the old country, their Portugal, to do that. And he loved he could bare everything to her, yet the serious side of all this, his voice hearing and Triple Suiter, had not been revealed. Maybe he could ease into it by making it appear humorous, then big it up, little by little, over time. He mentioned he told Drayton he had a guardian angel called Triple Suiter; that was a first. He had no idea she suspected more from observing him, but she did. It was what he said on the way to the hospital in his delirium that night Carlos shot him – calling out, over and over, for someone named Triple Suiter. His friend John Chrome knew all about Trip from the talks they'd had in the old days on acid. He wanted to tell her tonight about the slipper Trip saw in the gator's eye that day when he was fifteen, but he didn't. He was afraid she would think him crazy. The bad crazy, or the scary crazy. He'd have to give it more background and thought. But that aside, he could honestly tell her he loved her as he had a thousand times, and that was something Leda, his ex, would not allow. Some "too cool to go there" in the "above it all" thinking her populist, strong-woman thing watered back in the 60s. She'd claimed to be untouched by man/woman love. Just too, too cool to be in that position with someone, and she thought Aubrey ought to be above it with her. She played with other people, looking for souls she could talk down to that felt as hopeless as she did privately. Cry like a baby when he shaved her legs. Cry in bed when they tumbled. He had asked her if she slept with his friend Arquette. She denied it, and in terms of physical contact, that was true. Aubrey told her, "If you play me for a fool, I'll be very disappointed in you, and if I let you play me for one, I know you'll be very disappointed in me."

That last day, when she was packing her bags to go to Miami, he unloaded on her about her narcotic use. Told her he thought she was enslaved by it. Her answer was, "Yes, I guess that's the straight and narrow of it, Aubrey. I can't stay straight living here, and I've had enough of narrow in this town." He told her she should stay with him and go into rehab. That by leaving, she was burning down the barn to kill the rats. She said, "Living in this town, that would be the only way to kill the rats." When their marriage was legally over, for a number of what he considered reconcilable reasons – she didn't reconcile; she didn't try – she just stayed in Miami, away from him, and he knew it was because she felt safer alone.

Christaine went to bed. He sat on the porch. Triple Suiter came out on his arm in his loud, Jack Taylor, three-piece suit, lit up like a tube of Luminal, ready to listen.

"You have plenty to say about this, don't you, Trip?"

"Think so?"

Trip had been quieter since Drayton was old enough to talk. Aubrey hit on *him* lately for conversation more than the other way around, and sometimes Trip disappeared for days.

"I know Trip. I remember what you said that day I was in the water with The Dragon. I froze, but so did the gator for some reason, and you told me that you saw a slipper in his eye and stared it down, and that's why the gator let me live. I remember my father holding a rifle and the Richards brothers not believing it. They kept telling me how brave I was and how lucky I was that the gator left me alone, but I told them my guardian angel scared it away. It was really you, Trip. I was only fifteen. Still Catholic as hell and I thought you were just my guardian angel. The Richards brothers laughed at me for saying that, but my father, the *devout* Catholic, nodded his approval."

"Yes," Trip said. "It's been a long time since I saw the man in the eye of that creature, what, 1959, and he was dressed like

Captain Nemo in the good story, Captain Nemo, in your dream at the campsite the other night, Aubrey. Maybe it is true, and it *is* what's left of Monsieur Verne himself that has been trans-slipperated and is now part of that creature."

"Trans-slipperated? You make that word up?"

"Yes, I made that word up. It can be one of our private cryptonyms from now on, like the many others in our little personal lexicon. I could have used the word 'transmogrify' to describe him, but that has kind of a grotesque, humorous connotation, and this is serious stuff we're seeing out there on the creek. I've told you many times, Aubrey. People, even you, can become a slipper after you move from the smaller windmill into a larger one with a bigger breeze."

"You mean after I die. And after Mr. Vern died, that's what happened to him."

"Please, no necro tonight. I'm not up for it. I've just had a good day."

Aubrey went to bed. Took two Trazadones for sleep as always. He lay there waiting for the voices to come, the ones he heard at bedtime, asking him, begging him, to "Pick a film, any film," because he had that mind – film – this man from the beaches and backwoods of Florida. In the dark next to Christaine, something came into his staging area, something that throbbed him – an old movie, *Distant Drums*, about the Seminole wars. It starred Gary Cooper. He had seen it as a boy in 1954, and there were many scenes with Osceola and Tarzan-types fighting alligators in the water with a knife. He could imagine what it looked like when that gator grabbed Lane Richards out of the chair and carried him to the creek to steal his head, then left the rest of the body for the public to find. The Tin Snip Killer was like that – left kills for approval in junked refrigerators, the doors wide open, with "Ship in a Bottle" written on them in blood. *Osceola*, he thought, *what a party it's going to be around here over this gator thing. It'll be like the Tin Snip again. The whole county will be looking for Two-Toed Tom. And what about the man the Richards twins saw in the woods? Someone I knew? A store downtown?*

He went for sleep, to the mental theatre that straddled his conscious and subconscious he called the Trazadone Lounge. The tall usher took him. The throb came. "Get me *Distant Drums*," he mumbled.

"Yes, Aubrey," the voices said, and there he was with Gary Cooper in an Indian village, carrying a white flag for a sit-down with Osceola.

ANIMAL SLIPPERS

Chapter 9: THE MONSTERS AND THEIR SLIPPERS

Two days after the Richards twins' incident, everything came out in the paper, including the names of the rogue gators and the stories behind them. Law enforcement organized a hunt with licensed trappers and hopped-up civilians. Any big gator was shot at and some were killed. The first thing after a kill, they looked at the reptile's feet to see if any had only two toes on the left front. The bellies were cut open, looking for human parts, especially a head, but nothing came of it. People began calling them the Ghost Gators.

On a back creek area off the South Fork, the foreman of the Harris Ranch, Darnell Drinkard, was watching the ranch ponds after the incident and found two-toed gator tracks in the woods that led him to the bank of a twenty-five-acre fill pond. It had been created for the new overpass on I-95 that ran along the ranch's west border. Darnell went back to the main house and returned with his half-track swamp buggy pulling a bass boat behind it. He had his autistic brother with him, two other cowboys, and four sticks of dynamite usually used on pine stumps for clearing pasture.

Two-Toed Tom and The Dragon ran across each other right after Tom killed Lane Richards. Their slippers, Nemo and Osceola, decided to move the gators from the populated waterways of the creek into the dry pinewoods to get distance and obscurity from the law and hunters, and now they occupied the manmade fill pond on the ranch. Nemo was not happy with Osceola and Two-Toed Tom for killing Lane Richards in broad daylight, but he knew it was very personal for Osceola to have the head of the old gator hunter. Still, they usually consulted with each other before something like that was done.

The Dragon lay submerged in thick reeds with just his nose and eyes out of the water, but Two-Toed was spotted along the open part of a bank, half out of the water. Darnell, the foreman, knew when Tom saw them coming the gator would submerge, but they might be able to concuss him with the dynamite, and he'd float up dead or disoriented. He was right. Two-Toed left the bank and lay on the bottom in fifteen feet of water. He had air enough to stay there for a half hour before he had to move to another part of the pond, come up quick and grab air. He could do it again and again, until the men gave up. When he moved the first time, he caused air bubbles to rise. Darnell and the men saw it, got the bass boat in position over the top of him, and took a chance on the dynamite.

The first stick sent a shock through the water, and Two-Toed was stunned. In a confused spasm, he instinctively started to the top for air. When the second stick went off, it knocked him unconscious, and he rose and rolled over on the surface. One of the men in the boat cocked his 30-30, but Darnell said he wanted the gator alive, said he would be worth a fortune to any amusement park and not to tell anyone. If the sheriff or Fish and Game knew they had him, they would surely come and take him from them.

The men got hooks and ropes on the stunned gator and hauled him to the bank. Someone drove the mile and a half back to the ranch and got a forty-foot-long stock trailer. Tied and duct taped, the huge Two-Toed was dragged into the trailer with a come-along, then, cheering like Mideast fighters in the back of pickups, the men headed back to the main house on the ranch.

When it was dark, Captain Nemo walked The Dragon out of the pond and followed the belt tracks of Darnell's half-track for a mile, until he could see the buildings and lights of the grange. At two in the morning, he moved in. He was lucky Darnell brought the dogs inside, otherwise they would be barking all night at Tom tied inside the six-horse stock trailer, rattling the steel sides, thrashing, wanting out.

The Dragon moved up to the back of the low-slung rig and stood on his hind legs to remove the pin on the door with his mouth, but it was chained and padlocked. Around the side, Captain Nemo had him gently bite the tires, holding his teeth into the bite to let the air out slow and quiet. This lowered the trailer just enough that he could slowly tear out the bottom wood slats with his machine shop mouth. Darnell heard noises, but just thought it was Two-Toe banging his body.

When The Dragon got inside the trailer, he bit through the duct tape around the end of Two-Toed's jaws. Next, he tooth-sliced the ropes. Together, they left through the open hole in the side of the trailer, walking off the property through the dry woods until the house was a hundred yards behind them. Darnell woke when the trailer noise stopped and went out to check on Tom.

"Johnny! Quentin!" he yelled at the other house. "Get up! Somebody stole the gator. Get some horses tacked quick, and one a-you take a truck and head for the main gate to see if whoever it was is still here."

Darnell's autistic little brother, nicknamed Half Track after his brother's swamp buggy, nodded his head like a turkey. He wanted to go with the men and hunt for the thieves, but his brother told him no, and their aging mother held her upset son back.

Bill cap headlights showed between the ears of their horses, and two cow dogs followed them at a run. The gators' tracks and tail marks were obvious. In fifty yards, Darnell pulled his horse up and said to the other man, "Quintin, I'll be god damned if there ain't two sets a tracks here. Nobody took our gator. Another damn gator took our gator. Now you tell me how that's possible when we only put one in that stock trailer. Look at the ground here. Am I crazy?"

No biologist could have told them how it happened. It was something only a Seminole *yaholi* medicine man could explain, but not to a Southern Baptist.

The searchers went on, their lights on the ground, the dogs circling and barking. The Dragon and Two-Toed heard them coming and were still a hundred yards from a black mangrove trail into a creek. Gators are fast on dry land. They can run like a Jesus lizard if they want to. Between them, it was 1600 pounds of dinosaur throw-back crashing through palmettos and pine land scrub like something military and diesel. The dogs caught up. One grabbed The Dragon's tail thirty feet from the water. The Dragon slapped the dog off and the huge splash from the two of them sent spray ten feet in the air. They made it. The men pulled their horses up at the edge, the water still roiling, the tree limbs still moving back and forth.

Darnell took off his hat, leaned forward, and crossed his arms on top of his saddle horn. "And this, gentlemen, is why the army lost the Seminole war. Can't take a horse in there. Can hardly take a man."

Once out in the open water of the South Fork, the gators swam submerged for long distances, surfacing only when they had to for air then diving back down to keep going in the dark.

Chapter 10: STORY

"Last night, Daddy told you about Mr. Vern, the man from France who moved to the young alligator after the fight with the coon dog. The alligator, with the help of Mr. Vern, its slipper and guardian angel, grew to be big and strong. Mr. Vern's magical powers gave it an extra-hard skin called a hide. Then Mr. Vern made the bumps on its back, called scutes, stand up extra tall, and its head extra big and boney to protect it. Mr. Vern decided it would be fun to change his own name to Captain Nemo, just like the story he wrote that Daddy read you in the children's book this summer. Do you remember *20,000 Leagues under the Sea?*"

The boy nodded.

"Mr. Vern chose the name Nemo because in Latin, an old language, it means 'no man.' So from now on, in this story, we will call Mr. Vern 'Nemo,' because he moved into an alligator as a slipper and changed himself. Now he has a real living Nautilus, like the submarine in the story he wrote, okay?"

The boy nodded again. "What's a skoot, Daddy?"

"A scute. Scutes are the bony bumps like little fins down the center of an alligator's neck and back. Look there on the floor at your stuffed gator. Every alligator has one hundred and forty-four scutes, and The Dragon's were taller than any other gator's to scare his enemies away.

"One day, on the Loxahatchee River, Nemo was letting his gator feed on fish when a slipper who called himself Mr. Stilch entered the gator's mind from the nose of a big, soft-shell turtle. He told Nemo he had lived in lots of animals, and a long time ago he lived in a man named Trapper Nelson. Trapper knew many things about living on the rivers and in the woods, and Mr. Stilch learned a lot from him before he died. Then Mr. Stilch, being a slipper, moved on from Trapper to live in a big gar fish and after that, the soft-shell turtle. After telling Nemo his story, Mr. Stilch stayed with Captain Nemo and became his first mate on the alligator submarine, like the first mate on the Nautilus. Together they were clever about getting by and doing some of the things Nemo wanted to do to keep Florida a beautiful place for animals and people to live, just like the things he did to keep the world safe from the people who started wars in *20,000 Leagues under the Sea*."

Drayton climbed out of bed.

"Where are you going?"

"I want to ride my alligator with Captain Nemo and Mr. Stich."

"Not Stich." He tickled the boy. "That's Stilch, with an L."

"What's that name mean, Daddy?"

"Uh, I made it up. Let's just say my slipper told me to say that."

"What is *your* slipper's name, Daddy?"

"His name is Triple Suiter, because he always wears a dress suit with three parts – his pants, his vest, and jacket."

Drayton's eyes were wide and thinking. "What about Two-Toed Tom, Daddy, the other alligator in the story?"

"Tomorrow night I'll tell you about him. Turn the page. Finished."

"No, Daddy. What page? There's no book."

"It's an imaginary book we're reading, Drayton, remember?"

"But I want more."

"Tomorrow night, if you're a good boy for Mommy."

Aubrey pulled the covers over him and turned off the light.

"Daddy, my gator won't spank me back like I spank him, will he?"

"No. You can be his slipper and tell him to do what you say, like Captain Nemo does. Besides he's a stuffed gator, not a live one."

"Okay. Mansion! Goodnight, Daddy. Goodnight, Triple Suiter."

Aubrey laughed to himself and went downstairs to Christaine.

"Did he go to sleep?"

"Yep. He got a little excited about the story, but conked."

"I'd like to listen one night. You're not getting too scary for him, are you?"

"No, no, it's all PG stuff."

"So where are you getting this material for your children's story?"

"From me. My past. I was around my father's friends growing up, and we all hunted gators, quail, deer, hogs, snakes. When I was in my teens, those same two bull gators were out there, the giant ones you heard the deputy and the paper talking about."

"Are you using those for the story?"

"I mean, I'm actually taking some of this from the story told me by the Richards twins when I was a kid."

"Right."

"So, like you heard, there were other actual gator kills around here in the 70s, and these two gators they're all talking about were blamed. I mean, in ten years, three people, all grown men, were killed. One just disappeared. The funny thing was, every time it happened, the heads were bitten off the bodies and nowhere around. I mean, gators usually don't do that. They eat softer parts."

"Why is that funny?"

"I'm getting to that. The Richards, as I said before, were weird but kinda cool. They could spin cracker stories with the best of them, and even though they looked and acted like crackers, they were real educated crackers. Bookworms."

"Then that must be *some* story you are telling our son. I hope you're not scaring him to death."

"I find it ironic.Funny. I'm up there telling him a story about those gators, and this real stuff is going on now. I'm trying to soften it, although it's no worse than Jack and the Beanstalk or Hansel and Gretel when you look at the subtext in that old stuff. There's the good gator in the story, The Dragon, and Two-Toed's not all that bad. You can't blame Osceola or the Seminole nation for being sore about everything that happened to them."

"True, but Drayton is a little boy, remember."

"Yeah, I know, and I was thinking of making the tale more Bambi-like, putting in animals with less teeth. You remember that story you wrote for the magazine about an armadillo that could snap his toenails together and make fire in the woods? Well, I wanna add that to the story. In fact, I had a dream about these gators and your armadillo the last time I camped by the creek."

"Oh, great. I don't know, Aubrey. What if he starts to think burning the woods like the armadillo did in the story would be a lot of fun?"

"Well, it *is* good. The woods need to burn now and then. I'll keep the story in the realm of conservation. I'll have the gators only spank people with their tails, not eat them. He's gonna have to find out about these things sooner or later, though. What was the armadillo's name in your story?"

"Strike, like strike a match, and he was very careful to check which way da wind blows, so he didn't burn something down he shouldn't."

"Good. Strike it is, then, from Mommy's story. I'll tell him."

"I hope he doesn't think alligators are pets and try to get too close to one. I can't believe you got Henry to stuff that gator for him."

"Yeah, well, he loves it. The gator. And he loves to go out to Henry's place and look at the taxidermy."

"And what do you love?"

"You, and those scars on your upper lip. And those waterbed

eyes of yours that make me want to touch you in a place that can't be refused, and all the rest of you, white girl."

"Not so white. The Portugal part, remember?"

"I love that, too. That puts fire in our child from you, so he doesn't become a brooding Englishman like me. Come here." He put his arm around her. She lay her head over.

"You know, Aubrey, it's amazing we all lived through that Carlos thing. And it's amazing you are normal – well, mostly – after that bullet went through your head."

"What you mean mostly?" he grinned.

"You know how you are, talking to yourself all the time."

"I'm not talking to myself. I'm talking to a little man that lives in my armpit called a slipper. His name is Triple Suiter."

"You mean your armpit is named Slipper, and a little man named Triple Suiter lives in it, or the little man is a slipper? Why do you call him a slipper?"

"Oh, shut up. I don't know. Always have, after Reve he Gypsy lady told me that's what he was when I was a kid. Guess it's because he slips around in my head and my armpit and down my arm sometimes to dance. I also am fascinated by the term 'slip away.' I used to say 'slip away' in the old days on that drug, MDA, just as I got to the place when it titers the blood so called immaculate."

"And your armpit?"

"I told Drayton about it."

"Your armpit?"

"No. Forget it. Let's talk about something else."

"Okay. More fantasy then. Sometimes I fantasize about the metal plate they put in your head when we make love," she laughed.

"What?"

"Yeah, the plate becomes you in a private way, to me, I mean. You're my monster now, my Frankenstein. It's a hotplate."

"Hot outside tonight. Why don't we go get in the pool as nature made us, and I'll play the kingfish; take this fever tree of mine and synchronize swim with you till the sun comes up, my Portuguese *belle tournure*."

"Okay, kingfish. And I'll be an Ondine."

"What's that again?"

"A freshwater mermaid. They live in the waterfalls and streams of Germany instead of the ocean. Only I'll be a very different kind of Ondine."

"How?"

"A mansion Ondine. Whooo. The Queen Farmer of fever trees."

"You *are* mansion to me, you doe-eyed, split-lip woman, and always will be."

Chapter 11: OSCEOLA

"Did you brush your teeth? I don't read to little boys who don't brush their teeth."

"Yes, Daddy."

"Are you in bed?"

"Yes, sir. Almost."

"Okay. I'm comin up."

"Yay! Tell me about the other gator tonight. You promised."

"First, how do we begin the story every night? What's the first thing Daddy says?"

"Oh, you say, 'This is the tale of two alligators.' But what if it was an alligator with two tails?" He laughed and burped and got out of bed and sat on his stuffed alligator that Aubrey had bought him.

"Oh, you're a very funny, kid." Aubrey reached and put him in a headlock then knuckled his scalp until he screamed. "So here we go. This is the tale of two alligators, and tonight, here comes Two-Toed Tom, very different and more dangerous than all the other alligators around.

"For a long time, Tom lived far away in a place called Alabama. He had an accident once. He got his left front foot caught in a steel trap, had to pull it free, and now he only had two toes on that foot. He was also in trouble for trying to bite people and spank them with his tail. You know Daddy has always told you to be careful around the water and look out for their little eyes and noses that barely stick out." The boy nodded. "And to never go near the water unless Mommy and Daddy are with you."

The boy nodded again, reached behind, and spanked the stuffed gator he sat on. "Bad gator," he said.

"So everyone was mad at Two-Toed Tom, and they went out to find him for the bad things he did. Tom had some very close calls when he was being hunted in Alabama and North Florida, so he left to be safe. Into the Suwanee River he went, splash! And down through the lakes and dry land stretches to the big Kissimmee River. From there, he took the river south, going around every lock, all the way into the big lake they call Okeechobee, the liquid heart of Florida. Then, almost where he wanted to be, he ran into another big gator called Cattail. Cattail was famous for his skill with his tail, known to knock full grown cows off the bank with it into the water, and guess what?"

"What, Daddy, what?"

"Inside Cattail lived a slipper, and guess who it was?"

"Who?"

"The famous war chief of the Seminoles, Osceola, come back from the dead as a slipper to look for his head."

"What head?"

"The one he lost when he was in prison. Now he travelled around with Cattail looking for it so he could enter Indian heaven, because they won't let you in without a head."

"But if he doesn't have a head, how can he see where he's going?"

"No, that was as a human, silly. Of course, he has a head now as a slipper and guardian angel."

"Oh."

"Anyway, Osceola and Cattail decided they weren't going to let Two-Toed Tom pass through the section of the river where they lived, and a big fight happened."

"Who won?"

"Two-Toed was just too much for Cattail and sent him running after a long battle."

"Yay."

"Osceola was so impressed with Tom that he slipped through

Cattail's nose during the fight and into Tom's. Osceola was very happy to have this more powerful gator to guide and control, and he was the first slipper to ever live in Two-Toed Tom. Together they swam across the big lake to the St. Lucie Canal and went east through the locks into the South Fork of the St. Lucie River. Our river."

"What's a lock?"

"A lock is a place where the water can't go through. It gets all stopped up like the bathtub you take a bath in, unless you pull the plug."

"Tell me some more."

"Well, soon, Tom and Osceola ran into The Dragon and Captain Nemo. At first, they thought there would be a fight, but Captain Nemo walked out on The Dragon's nose and offered to talk with Osceola. The two became good friends and decided to be partners and travel together. One day, they met an armadillo named Strike. Nemo decided to send his first mate, Mr. Stilch, out of The Dragon's nose into the armadillo's to speak with the Gypsy lady who rode inside the eyes of the creature. She was the armadillo's slipper and told the armadillo what to do. When Mr. Stilch came back, he said the Gypsy lady had just come to the armadillo from her other host, a coach whip snake, and that she moved back and forth between the two, each animal delivering her to the other as she requested. She told Mr. Stilch, the first mate, that the armadillo spent his day searching the soil for tender things to eat and that he should remember the creature also had an unusual talent."

"What's talent, Daddy?"

"Means he could do something no one else could do."

"What could he do?"

"He could strike his toenails together and make a fire, and that's why all the other armadillos called him Strike. The Gypsy lady said the humans were clearing land for houses where the armadillo lived, and he was sad and didn't know where he would live now. Mr. Stilch told her he would speak to Captain Nemo and Osceola, and they would meet her at this same place tomorrow and find a new place for the armadillo to live.

"Tomorrow night I'll tell you more, okay? Turn the page and go to sleep now. Slip away. Finished."

PART TWO

Chapter 12: THE DEVELOPER

His name was AM Sermon. The joke was, AM stood for amoral, not the morning hours or anything else. He had made a fortune gaslighting the many "As seen on T.V." items—super glues, food choppers, nose hair trimmers, and his favorite, a baldness cure made from johoba oil and a little lanolin. AM liked to think he ran things like a general.

His idols as a younger man were two brothers, Julius and Leonard Rosen, who also made their fortune with a baldness tonic, *all* lanolin – the oil sheep produce in their wool. The Rosen brothers' slogan was, "Have you ever seen a bald sheep?" So AM came up with, "Have you ever seen a bald Indian?" as in American Indian, because his tonic came from plants in the Southwest, and he claimed the Indians massaged their scalps with and that's why they seemed to have a lot of hair.

The next thing of the Rosens' AM wanted to imitate was their success in land development. In the 1970s, the Rosens owned a huge project in Florida called Golden Gate, an endeavor famous for chicanery and hoodwink sales tactics and its predisposition to Ponzi; a project that in the end, went into bankruptcy, but AM, though he had somewhat the same reputation in his TV business, was out to convince everyone he was a plain dealer and honest, and that he would be the best developer ever to cross the St. Marys River and end up two hundred and fifty miles south in Martin County on the east coast, a talked-about and overlooked place, spider-veined with rivers, creeks, and waterfront property. The little town of Stuart, the county seat, was called the Sailfish Capital of the World.

AM knew you couldn't develop property without getting dirt under your nails, not arm and hammer dirt like the Richards twins said, but white-collar dirt, acceptable, venial dirt in a society that admires money. So he took on a partner, a man from a family of influence in North Carolina who he had grown up and gone to school with. He and the man were in the same fraternity at Guilford College, in Greensboro. His name was Jim Lovill, a physically large man known as Big Jim. Big Jim's daddy was made by moonshine and bootleg cigarettes in the first and middle parts of the twentieth century. Today, the business had branched into strong arm, Tar Heel monopolies like milk trucks, tobacco warehouses, heating oil, stolen cars, and some narcotics; the Lovill family needed to get money into circulation, and there was no better way than to glom onto a construction project and feed cash to it, then get it back double in the end.

"If it please the commissioners, I present you a plan that will not only improve the beauty of your county, but increase your tax base significantly," out-of-towner AM Sermon told the panel. "Some of you know my intentions, but today you will see renderings of the future home of four thousand residents in a place bordered by natural beauty, existing in harmony with its surroundings. Members of the commission, I give you Cypress Prairie."

Alfred Murrow Sermon, from Greensboro, pulled the sheet off the architectural model of a golf course, clubhouse, and residential homes that resembled the scale of a child's electric train landscape. The project ran along a creek off the St. Lucie River and butted up against the Z Bar Up, a ranch owned by the Zarnitz family. The head of the Zarnitz family, old Caspar Zarnitz, had his two sons running the spread, and he was none too happy about houses seemingly dropped from the sky onto the land next to his, even though it made his land more valuable. He didn't need the money; he thought like the dead Richards twins thought. He just wanted the lifestyle.

The sons were brands of the old man. They hired lawyers and wrote negative editorials during the county commission's long review of the project opposing its approval. It changed nothing. The commissioners, all but one, wanted the revenue from the new tax base and voted for it. Now it was war.

Aubrey was a long-time friend of the Zarnitz family. He camped alone along the creek on their ranch once a month to clear his head and add things to it. This was where he had the dream about the animals and talking slippers in a circle around him.

"Can I take that same mare tonight?" he said on the phone to Sam Zarnitz.

"Sure. I'll tell Emilio to keep her in after they feed."

He got to the ranch around six o'clock in the afternoon and rode a mile and a half to his spot along the creek. He hung up a hay net, tied out the mare, and built a fire in the same place thirty feet in from the water. The mosquitos were out, so Aubrey went to the creek and found some hardened sap on the trunk of a black mangrove tree and cut it off with a hatchet. Back at his camp, he put pieces of the sap in his fire to create a smudge, a common backwoods mosquito repellent, then set about cooking something and downing a drink. "It's been a good life," he thought. *"Some of it real. Small parts, maybe a little, fake."*

"And just what parts were fake? You think it is over? Your life? You are all of fifty." It was Triple Suiter, his slipper.

"Where you been?"

"Dictating my new book to Amper Sand, who, as you know, sits in the bone bowl of my chest, the wizard of Underwood

typewriters and my own grand slipper. He is a never-ending re-
minder to the world of the word *and*. Nothing ever stays the same,
and there is always what's next. You can say *and* after anything
eternally. Ampersand."

"*And* I'd like to read that stuff he types sometime."

"Sorry, my amanuensis hides the manuscript, written back-
wards, only to be read in a mirror."

"I know, I know. I've heard it all before. That's some weirdness."

"Not to me. Mankind."

"No, Trip, listen. Sometimes I wish I was, what? Wiser, more
mature, instead of all this theatre I do. That's what I meant when
I said 'fake.'"

"But I like your theatre, Aubrey."

"Yeah, but when it comes to responsibility, I mean, am I okay
as a parent? And I'll never know how I ran that big car dealership
without my mom after I bought it from her. She was much more
pragmatic and level-headed than me. But I did run it for years until
I sold it, so I could run away with this life of mine. I was lucky.
Just lucky. Now I think I should be doing something more arm and
hammer."

"You'll figure out something to get you busy soon. No, you were
good at the business and got a lot of respect from your competition
and employees. Your employees liked you – well, not all of them –
but what did the man, whoever the man was, say about that?"

"What?"

"He said, 'I don't know what the secret to success is, but I do
know the secret to failure, and that is trying to please everyone.'"

"Yeah. Hand wash tumble dry that."

"Now, Aubrey, I don't know if I would get this close to the
water with this campsite of yours tonight. You might see the great
alligators, the armadillo, and the coach whip in another dream.

And you can be assured they will have that tribe of slippers like me with them, the ones that give those long, idealistic speeches and encomiums about the past." Trip making fun of him.

"Maybe, but I kinda enjoyed that last time. I'm gonna make one more drink, sit back, and get into the night. Think about the future, the projectamenta, as John Chrome calls it."

He put wood and more mangrove sap on the fire and backed away. A blue heron leaving the creek bank when the fire went higher squawked and bitched, like they always do. A snook hit something with that give-away boom sound in the water, and then it was back to just a single mullet jumping now and then and a single splash. He heard bull frogs and noise from an ibis rookery across the creek. There were some cattle egrets mixed in with the ibis, he could tell, because they made that croaking sound like a baby gator. A bull bellowed somewhere out on the Zarnitz ranch. He remembered growing up on quarter horses and working cattle all the time when he was a boy and a young man.

"There is a young cowboy; he lives on the range. His horse and his cattle are his only companion. Good night, you moonlight ladies. Rock-a-bye, sweet baby Aubrey, sweet..."

"What? Jesus jumping roadkill crosses! That song doesn't work with your name in it. 'Good night, sweet baby Aubrey'? What are you going to rhyme with next? Tawdry? You're not James Taylor!" Trip said, sliding down on Aubrey's arm.

"I know, I know. It's just I love that song, and I go to cow pens, quick horses, and sleeping in the woods like I used to when I hear it."

"I remember. I know you miss those days. I didn't mean to..."

"Well, who was that other band? The weird one I liked that came out with James Taylor at the concert that night twenty years ago."

"It was," said Trip, laughing, "Lothar and the Hand People."

"Shit, yes. That was them." And now they both were laughing. "Who could forget a band with a name like Lothar and the Hand People? That's as good as The Dead Kennedys or Root Boy Slim and the Sex Change Band."

They talked and talked until Aubrey stood up and led the mare down to the creek for a drink of water. He looked hard at the surface first with his flashlight for red gator eyes, then shined the light around the banks, looking for other eyes.

He tied the mare back to the tree and gave her more hay. Two more sticks on the fire, and he put a horsehair rope off his saddle around his sleeping bag – superstition in cow country about rattlesnakes not crossing the rope. The fire burned down. He almost fell asleep when Trip showed again and reminded him to take his Trazadone pill. The voices came after that like they usually do, begging him, "Pick a film, Aubrey, any film."

"I haven't seen *Two-Lane Black Top* in a while. Forever. James Taylor's in it. He's driving a tricked-out Chevy cross country in some kind of race with another guy. I saw it in '71."

"Yes, Aubrey," the voices said, and down he slid to the Trazadone Lounge, to the anteroom of dreams, where he got in that bad car with Sweet Baby James and drove west in the sky out over cattle country, talking and looking down at the great herds on the pangola prairie, a "big moon sinking from the weight of the load."

5:30AM came. Mourning doves and eternally pissed off mockingbirds started early. A coon made a noise licking the plate of eaten supper. It woke him. The coon ran. He went back to sleep, he thought, but the demi-dream came, the half sleep, and it started to happen. He thought the noise was the coon coming back, but it was the animals – the big gators, the armadillo, and the coach whip with their slippers, walking up around his fire circle. Triple Suiter went down Aubrey's exposed arm and joined the group, just like before. Aubrey's eyelids went clear again.

"This cannot be permitted to go forward, my friends," Captain Nemo said in a French accent from the nose of his huge gator. "Sermon and his housing project are creating lesions in the earth to fatten his obsession as *le grifteur*. There are many species of animal and plants on this land he is hiding from the inspectors. The sand ridge on the property is home to the endangered gopher tortoise, and my fellow man, Monsieur Audubon, who comes from the same town in France as me, would turn in his grave to know Sermon plans to destroy the habitat of the endangered red cockade woodpecker before authorities discover the bird is there."

"We attack them. Run them off this land. These are cruel people," the grand slipper Osceola said from *his* gator's nose, the terrifying Two-Toed Tom.

"I have my armadillo to burn them out," Martha the Gypsy lady suggested. "My coach whip snake can unlock any door or gate with his prehensile tongue."

Aubrey took a big breath and coughed twice. That woke him, and nothing was there except his horse over by the tree.

A *dream*, he thought. Same one again, but it seemed real. There's no way it was real. That mare would have broken her halter if gators were this close. He got to his knees and shook his head. Chewed the inside of his cheek flesh. Walked to the creek bank, and there it was, a big two-toed track at the edge in the white sand, and next to that, another set of tracks. He shook for a second, then picked up his camp, saddled the mare, and rode a mile and a half in a dog trot back to the main house and barns.

On the way home, he called for Trip's attention, and Trip came.

"Did you see any of that dream, Trip?"

"What, *Two-Lane Black Top*? Yes, Amper Sand and I watched the film with you. I like the part..."

"No, the other dream! The one I had before I woke up this morning."

"I did see all of that, because I got up early myself and was working on my book."

"Trip, I watched you go down my arm to those other slippers like you did a month ago, and there were the big gators, the armadillo and snake, and the rest of the Disney shit-show. Then of all things, I go down to the creek and there's Two-Toed Tom-tracks on the bank. I could have been had if it wasn't a dream."

"Well, which was it?"

"Don't know. Just don't know."

"Maybe you were still dreaming when you went to the creek. Maybe the tracks were a dream."

But Trip knew. He just wasn't going to reveal everything this early. Soon Aubrey would become part of it; the dream was almost over. The animals and their slippers were starting to warm up to the man who now and then invaded their meeting place to spend the night.

The old snowbird Yankees talked and talked on benches downtown like they had forever. The recent alligator kill was a popular topic. People hide it, but it's true; they like atrocity. There had been vandalism on Sermon's new development that made the papers, too. The heavy equipment had tires cut, and sugar had been put in fuel tanks. The Zarnitz boys were suspects. They even said maybe they did it and dared the county to prove it or do anything about it.

Chapter 13: CONFRONTATION

"You ready, Drayton? Get your hat and headlight. I got the gigs. We're gonna get the big frogs tonight, boy, then Momma's gonna cook us some frog legs."

"*Big* frogs, Daddy!"

"That's right. Frogs throw up when they hear our names. He we go!"

Before Aubrey slipped the john boat off the trailer at the landing and lifted his son onto the seat in front of him, Deputy Kimmel pulled up in his unmarked patrol car.

"Evening, Aubrey. You boys froggin or fishin?"

"Tonight, it's frogs, Detective."

"I see you have some good help with you."

"Yep, well, we'll see about that. It's his first time."

"Had any thoughts about that story Shane Richards told the veterinarian? Any idea who that man might have been, the one he saw burying the refrigerator who owned a store downtown?"

"It's been plenty on my mind, but for the life of me, I can't put a name to him."

"Well, let me know if you do. You know how to find me. If you see any big gators tonight, especially one with only two toes on a front foot, run like hell, then call the wildlife people." He grinned.

Aubrey and Drayton went a mile down the creek in the boat and turned off to a narrow place in the reeds that led to a hidden pond. It got shallow. He cut his motor and poled in with the outboard pulled up on the transom and locked it in place, moving quiet with the pole to a pocket where the lily pads covered the surface. Frog World.

"Okay, Drayton. Reach up and turn on your headlight. Look for the little gold eyes. Take this gig and hold it in front of you. There's one right there. Get him," Aubrey whispered. "Good shot. Bring him in the boat and let Daddy take it off the gig."

"I want to take it off. Owee!"

"Take it off and put it in the bag then."

"Owee!"

"Come on, cowboy, get that frog off there. You're gonna prick your fingers now and then, so be tough. You wanted to. Good job. Now put him in the bag and get another one."

They circled around for a half hour, looking for bull frogs until the bag was almost full. The lily pads got thicker in one spot, and Drayton was going to take his turn at a big shining red eye when it disappeared. It wasn't a frog. Aubrey felt the water move under the john boat and thought, *Manatee, I hope, and not what I think that was*. He told his son to be still and quiet. When the gator came up twenty feet from the boat, it let its tail and back breech the water, as if to show Aubrey it was longer than the boat.

"Now, Drayton, be real still. There's an alligator just off the left side.

Daddy's gonna make it go away, and then we are gonna go, because I think we have more than enough frogs."

Drayton turned around and looked anyway. His mouth opened, and stayed open when he saw it. Aubrey tried to turn the boat away from the gator, and the thing swam to the front of the boat and bumped it. He was shocked. They won't do that. *They leave you alone unless you have a small animal jumping around or a fish on*, he thought. The gator circled around and swam closer.

"Look, Daddy, The Dragon and Captain Nemo." The high scutes were visible along the back, and so was the extra-large head and bone ridge nose.

Wanting to keep his child thinking about anything but danger, he said, "Yes, that looks like Nemo's gator, The Dragon. Hi, Mr. Dragon."

"Hi, Captain Nemo," Drayton imitated.

With the inner voice, Aubrey said, "Trip. Come here now!"

"I'm here. I was enjoying the frog hunt, Aubrey. Scary as it seems, move the boat closer and let me see the alligator's eye better." Instead, Aubrey cranked the engine and gunned the boat forward, running it up on a mud bank he couldn't see under the shallow water.

He told Drayton not to make a sound, that Daddy was going to scare the gator away.

"Ah, yes. Guess who. There stands the beautiful man, Captain Nemo, in full old-time portrait attire. He sees me now," Trip said.

"What's he doing? I've got my hand on my 9mm, and I'll use it if I have to."

"Don't do that, Head Wound," Trip said. "He sees me. Don't cock the gun or let him see it. Nemo is a man of reason and compassion."

By the bank, the water trailed another big head, and then the head stopped and stared.

"Now there's two of them. Damn it."

"Yes, Aubrey, and I suspect that's Osceola with his intrepid beast, Two-Toed Tom. I suggest you cut the motor."

"I'll shoot him, I swear. I'll kill him, but I'm not killing this motor."

"Let's maintain our composure here, Aubrey, because Nemo just smiled and nodded to me. They are not going to do us any harm."

"I still want *us* and my child out of here. What about I throw some frog meat in the water and leave?"

"I think that would be a nice gesture. Just throw a few at each of them."

Aubrey did. The gators opened their mouths for more and got them. Aubrey put the motor in reverse, but it was not enough to get the john boat off the mud bar. He shut the motor down and tried with the pole. Out of the corner of his eye he saw The Dragon move to the other side, then go toward the bow and come partially out of the water onto the bar. He put one hand on Drayton's shoulder and the other on the gun that he held below the boat's gunnel. Then something happened he thought would happen only in Hollywood – the gator turned his huge head against the bow and pushed the boat off the mud bar, freeing it.

They slid into deeper water. Aubrey looked to his left to see where Osceola and Tom were again. Trip said, "You see? I think they are both on our side. Throw them more frogs, and then we can leave."

Aubrey did and poled the boat out of the shallow pocket. On the open water at full speed, he asked, "How can what happened in there be true, Trip?"

"You saw it. You are not camped by the creek in a Trazadone movie this time."

"That tells me you know every detail of those two dreams and why they happened and what they really are. Are you the architect of all this?" Aubrey asked, mad.

"Only as a minor adjunct to Nemo. That place happens to be their regular meeting place. The first night you were there, Two-Toed Tom was going to kill you. I stopped it when Osceola saw me come out on your arm while you were asleep. Two-Toed went back in the water and came back an hour later with the whole coterie: The Dragon, the armadillo, the coach whip snake, and their slippers. I advise you not to say anything to anyone, even to John Chrome, whom you like to tell everything to when you are imbibing psycho chemicals on the beach together looking for Jesus. In this case, not only will any member of the public think you are Peter Cracked-Head Pan, so will an educated, open-minded expansionist like John Chrome. Turn the page. Finished."

"So everything was true. No dream. I saw those people with the animals at the camp and I guess I couldn't see them tonight in the gators' eyes because I was too scared and excited. Thanks for fucking with my head."

"Yes. Probably. They are not hallucinations or religious apparitions, Aubrey. You are not in a dream state now, nor were you completely in a dream at the campsite. You had, I'd say, the 'half-moon syndrome.' One foot on the light side, the other on the dark side of that moon you and Pink Floyd sing about all the time in the tabernacle of your truck. You are actually able to see things like this, like I can, if you concentrate, especially after what that bullet of late did to your bronco brain. The Latin words for this are *ultima thule*. You are seeing out to one of the farthest horizons of reality. There're some words in German for that, too, but I can't think of them right now. You were able to see Nemo at fifteen years old when you waded into the water with him years ago. You were more receptive to it at that age, when the imagination is so open and large, and not so slot-car mature yet. Your brain is trying to tell you that, by slowly introducing it to your conscious side, using those demi dreams you have at the campsite. This is not imagination. It is a reality of a rare and mostly unknown kind. You and I need to go back to the campsite soon. You have to try harder to stay completely awake so you are convinced you can see the slippers in the eyes and on the nose of those alligator gun boats."

"But I was looking at the dream and the speeches they gave as a kind of unreliable allegory. I mean, I can accept small amounts of supernatural. For example, for the sake of the story, I had no trouble with the supernatural size of Sissy Hankshaw's thumbs in *Even Cowgirls Get the Blues*."

"You will have to take your acceptance of the supernatural a lot further with this, Aubrey. This is way past Sissy's long thumbs. You have heard me say that slippers sometimes move to and live in animals. There is some beautiful verse by the Roman poet Ovid in *Metamorphosis*, 'The spirit wanders, comes now here, now there, and occupies whatever frame it pleases. From beasts it passes into human body and from our bodies into beasts, but never perishes.'"

"Shit, this is something," Aubrey said out loud in the boat, instead of in the inner voice.

"Momma says don't say that word," Drayton said, grinning and un-phased by what just happened, delighted to see the big alligators from the story his daddy told him at bedtime. He told his mother everything when they got home, and Aubrey just sat drinking a gin, smiling and winking at Christaine, not knowing what to say while she mixed the puzzled look with one of approval, because it was her child's own story and it was a good one, the coinage a budding writer would bring.

~

Now he will not wait. Not after what happened on the frog hunt, and what he wants to see in those ancient eyes of theirs, those creatures whose species is two million years old.

He makes the arrangement for the horse he takes to the camp each time. It is getting dark when he arrives at the creek, so he hurries to tie out the mare and set up his fire. He will do everything the same – sit by the fire, have his two drinks, and do some thinking, but it will be hard to think about anything else. He might sing more James Taylor to relax.

"Trip?"

"What?"

"Can we do this now, instead of right before sunrise?"

"Nemo and Osceola hunt their alligators for food this time of night, so even though they live right in this pocket of the creek, it is a long creek. This will not happen until five in the morning. We will see them when they come back from hunting. Take another half of that Trazadone pill before you get into your sleeping bag."

Aubrey led the mare down to the edge of the water to drink. This time, the grass was coming in strong behind the campsite. She was used to hobbles, so he turned her loose, hobbled, to graze all night.

Five in the morning came, grey at first, then pink to blue, and the same coon was back fooling with food bags. Aubrey woke, and Trip was right there. "Here they come," Trip said.

The gators walked out of the water like metal amphibians designed by the navy – leviathan, much bigger out of the water, when all of their size could be seen. Along the bank came the armadillo and the coach whip; all took their places around the burned-out fire pit.

"What are we going to do for the kingdom, our kingdom, and everyone's kingdom? We shall be *le intercessors*. We condemn them, *ipso facto*, by the very nature of the sins they commit," Nemo said from the wide snout of his submersible.

"We are going to raise hell, that's what," Osceola said. The Gypsy lady nodded. "Oh, and welcome, Aubrey Shallcross. It is good you can be with us this time, fully awake, and know you are with us." A laugh came up from the slippers.

"Thank you," Aubrey said. "This is new to me, but I am honored. I mean, all red and swoll up by what I thought could be only an illusory experience, some kind of head shaking story that has turned out *not* to be an illusion at all. I have suspended my disbelief, I promise you."

"And *we* are honored, Aubrey, to speak with another form like you again, a form that we all occupied at one time. Before I begin, allow me to say something." Nemo cleared his throat, preparing for one of his more oracular speeches, since Aubrey was truly awake and part of this now.

"*J'aimerais dire*…oh, forgive me. I slipped into my other tongue. In English, of course. At this time in history, the world is in a dangerous form of reduction, losing species after species every decade, a cascade depletion effect – not only primary animals in the chain, but animals whose secondary life depends on the existence of primary ones. At this time in history, it is known, if you totaled the immense weight of all the mammals in the world, man and the livestock man owns would account for 95% of the weight, and what's left of the wild mammals would account for only 5%. Imagine what it was once. The birds, even the insects, are disappearing. Two hundred years ago, the sky would blacken for three whole days from bird migrations. Ships were stopped dead in the water by huge schools of fish, unable to move for hours. This planet is on a death march. We can try to make a difference, and if we don't, and that is possible, we can say at least we fought for it." Nemo bowed his head.

"Bravo, bravo!" the group yelled.

"Now," Nemo continued, "the business tonight. We have sworn to do the common good, preventing projects the county has approved, such as building homes on sensitive sites – the 'poison projects,' we call them." They all rumbled their little voices, like the English Parliament. "Monsieur Sermon, whose project is called Cypress Prairie, has nefariously skirted the truth of good conscience. He is burying gopher tortoises alive and cutting down red cockade woodpecker nests. Both of these are endangered species. He digs ponds dangerously deep above the sacred aquifer, for fill to build his roads. Highly illegal and destructive. He paid off a land evaluation company to deny that his project blocks the essential sheet flow of water from the wetlands west towards the St. Lucie River, which will change the ecology of the area. I say we gather this week and expose him. Catch him killing the gophers and birds and commit a crime of our own for the common good. We will use our resources to punch through to the aquifer below his ponds and get him fined, maybe jailed! The holes we punch are a temporary evil, will land him in front of a judge if we are lucky, and can be repaired later. A resounding "yay" came from the group. "I don't believe in shutting down every project. Mankind must live somewhere, but they must find *le equipoise*, a certain balance with the natural world they stupidly don't realize they need. Badly planned, unnecessary projects in the wrong places should be stopped, especially when it is only about money." Another cheer from group.

"How can I help?" Aubrey asked.

"In many ways," Nemo said. "We will let you know. We already receive help from the Seminole Freddie Tommie."

Aubrey couldn't believe it. "I've met him a couple of times. He was my friend The Junior's squad mate in Vietnam. How does he help you?"

Osceola answered. "He, like you, believes in the democracy of the dead. That would be us, the revenants, the 'slippers,' you call them, Aubrey. He, like you, knows things about nature through a medium like his *yaholi*, Billie Monday, *le griot*, as my colleague Monsieur Nemo would call him. He lives both on the land and in the water. You, Aubrey, have the wise and ancient

Triple Suiter to guide you and provide you with wisdom about these things. This will be a great help to us when we need you."

"How will you let me know?"

"I will come to you in the coach whip when they tell me to," the gypsy lady Martha said. "My snake can cover miles of ground. He flies over the sand and through the scrub at many miles per hour. I will have Two-Toed Tom or The Dragon bring me in their mouth across the river to your side, and then I'll go to your house with a message."

"And again, there is Freddie Tommie," Nemo said. "He is very accessible to us. Now you must excuse me and my dear army; we need to go to the other side of the creek today and plan how to disrupt the Cypress Prairie project before the building department approves the next phase. Good evening to you, Aubrey, and to you, Triple Suiter."

"Is there a Mr. Stilch on board The Dragon with you, Captain Nemo, acting as your first mate? If there is, I haven't met him yet," Aubrey said.

"No. No Mr. Stilch."

"Oh, I guess that's just someone I made up for my son's bedtime story. Good night."

Nemo smiled at him.

Chapter 14: SPEEDY AND ROBERTA

For money, Speedy Tanks rode a motorcycle inside the Globe of Death. He did wonders upside down on the steel mesh, the tires held only by centrifugal force and his nerve. The carnival he is with camps for the winter season along the creek off the St. Lucie River.

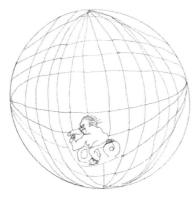

Speedy is married to Roberta, the Woman with No Legs, and when he caught her fooling around on him last year, he took the two snakes from her show, a young python and a coach whip, and threw them into the Florida woods. Roberta loved her snakes and her show, but to save the marriage, she let them go. To bandage things further, she brought Speedy The Girl with No Joints, and paid her to do certain shapes with him all night, breakfast included, knowing Speedy liked to get as close to that girl part as possible with nothing in the way, probably why he married Roberta.

The coach whip Speedy threw in the woods had been trained to wrap itself around an audience member's feet and softly whip them with its tail for food and applause. The python didn't have to do much more than just be there. The show people used to say, "Roberta can train anything." Once she trained a rat to dance and named him, Snitch. She would open her act with the rat, then the snakes, and a quart of words that changed the face on every ticket—"Beware the coach whip snake, thin and strong. You cannot catch it but it can catch you, the fastest one on earth. I have seen them since I was a child, their tan bodies, yellow eyes, black heads like Indians in war paint—that head held a foot off the ground while the rest of them flies over the sand. For centuries, the brothers and sisters of this eight-foot wonder have hypnotized and suckled the teats of cows and nursing women for their love of milk, their tail stuck in the baby's mouth to keep it quiet while they drained a breast." A gasp from the crowd. "You can tell when they've been around. The babies in town, start to get thin."

Roberta missed her old coach whip, and she missed talking to the Gypsy lady who inhabited the snake. Roberta was like Aubrey, a voice hearer, and she had a slipper of her own. There was no slipper living in the python, considered by slippers a boring animal, sleepy and slow, a creature who only stirred to eat.

One day, the python Speedy threw in the woods swallowed a tiny man from Guatemala. The man called out for his mother and God as buckles, coins, a flashlight, and his sneakers went in. No one knew what happened to the small soul. The python didn't feed for a month.

Unable to remain so anonymous was the coach whip. Martha, the snake's slipper, saw a young boy kneeling over a gopher tortoise hole and thought she could have her snake take two turns around his legs and the boy would feed it like Roberta did in the carnival. The boy screamed, wet his pants, ran home, and told his mother, but the mother didn't believe him and scolded him for making up a story because he couldn't make it to the bathroom. Martha and the coach whip lived in the gopher tortoise hole after that, and it was she who introduced the coach whip to The Dragon, Two-Toed Tom, and the armadillo Aubrey called Strike.

The county fair was on. Aubrey, Christaine, and Drayton were at one of Roberta's shows. Roberta had replaced the two snakes a year ago with two of the same after Speedy forgave her. Speedy picked her up and put her on her tall backed stool for the crowd to show off the fact she had only a pelvis without the rest of normal. She asked for a volunteer for the snake act and no one wanted to go up until Aubrey, the Florida boy who grew up with snakes, raised his hand. They didn't worry him much, but when he saw the coach whip, it reminded him of the animals by the campfire and the snake with the Gypsy woman who claimed her snake could get into anywhere by picking locks with its tongue.

He went blank on stage for a second, staring into the coach whip's eyes, looking for someone, another slipper. He turned his head so he could look in the python's eyes, too. Roberta tapped his shoulder with the microphone to get his attention back. She saw what he was doing with her snakes; no one she'd brought up to the stage before had done that. They were too afraid to put their faces in there. Now she seemed as distracted as Aubrey, but she went through the act she had performed a thousand times.

First, Roberta showed how friendly her new python was by throwing it over Aubrey's shoulders, then she placed her new coach whip at his feet and let it smell the meat on her hands. The coach whip took two turns around Aubrey's lower legs. Back and forth it whipped his legs, but gently, not hard like the folk legend says they do. He pretended the snake was hurting him to help the act. As he stood there, the python around his neck, watching the coach whip's tongue go in and out, he wondered if the snake really could pick a lock with its tongue like Martha said. He bent down and looked right in the snake's eyes again. Roberta watched him curiously. Drayton and Christaine's own eyes were big as babies over the snake act. The crowd loved it. Roberta charged ten dollars for anyone who wanted a photograph of themselves with the snakes.

Aubrey and Christaine talked to Speedy and Roberta after the show and invited them out to the farm for dinner. Speedy was flattered because locals usually wanted nothing to do socially with show people. "I look forward to dinner and to talking with you," Roberta said. "I saw you looking for something in my snake's eyes. I know about things like that."

When they sat down two nights later at the farm, Speedy spoke. "I met some people that knew you, Aubrey, and they described a house with a slide, murals, and mannequins all dressed up, but this is not it, is it?"

"No. I closed that house and moved to this one." Nothing more was said about the strange house up in the woods.

Christaine made picadillo for dinner: rice with spiced ground meat, onions, pine nuts, water chestnuts, parsley, and habanero peppers. Aubrey cut a swamp cabbage from the top of a ten-foot tree for a hearts of palm salad. They drank *caipirinhas*, a Brazilian drink made with the country's national spirit, *cachaca*.

"All right," Christaine said, "for dessert, if you want dessert, we have vanilla ice cream with sliced banana mangoes from the old Shallcross homestead on the St. Lucie River in Stuart or a Crème de menthe parfait."

Speedy carried Roberta out to the porch. Aubrey joined them. Speedy went back inside to help Christaine with the dishes.

"I want to tell you something, Aubrey," Roberta said. "Maybe I'm wrong, but I saw you looking for something in my snakes' eyes when you were on stage two nights ago. You probably didn't think I would notice, because if you are who and what I think you are, you think there is no one else quite like you. And if I am right, you are what the gypsies in the carnival call *drabarav*, a reader. Not of books so much, but a seer, and you see what I see in certain eyes."

"I know that word. The love of my life by the sink inside knows it, too. I know exactly what it means."

"Christaine is Gypsy?"

"Not really. Her father, Asante, speaks their language sometimes, and four other languages. Christaine and her sister inherited the polyglot gift."

"You're not all country boy, are you?"

"At heart, but no, I've been worked on by education. I don't use it much when I speak, but when the King wants it, I know how to call on it."

"Aubrey, did you see anything in my snake's eyes?"

"Only in the coach whip's, then it grinned and went away."

"That was a figurine you saw. His name is Roy. Figurines love to occupy coach whips. Roy told me once that they are so fast on the ground, it's like a riding a dirt bike."

"Figurine?"

"You saw it, didn't you? My other coach whip, the one Speedy threw in the woods, had a figurine inside it, too, named Martha."

Aubrey jerked a little when he heard this, but he didn't say anything about knowing Martha. "Yes, I saw him, your Roy. I don't call them figurines. I call them slippers."

"Interesting. Why?"

"Because they slip around minds, but not everyone can hear or see them, and they seem to slip to other people and creatures, too. And when they talk with you, they make you kind of slip away with them. They're not acceptable to regular people, even though regular people believe in vampires, werewolves, chupacabras, and skunk apes. Weird, huh?"

"I know. And I think you and I are going to be very good friends." Speedy and Christaine came out on the porch and sat with them until all the food made everyone sleepy. Speedy and Roberta went home.

Aubrey visited the carnival grounds sometimes once a week, and Roberta and Speedy came out to the farm a lot for drinks and laughs. One afternoon, watching Speedy practice in the Globe of Death, Aubrey told Roberta about the menagerie he encountered by the campfire and their apparition abilities, appearing in one place and vanishing to another. Roberta was bursting about it. He told her he met her Martha there with the coach whip and that she had an armadillo now.

"How did I find you, Aubrey Shallcross? I've always wanted to see such a thing. I told Speedy they were out there by the numbers, everywhere – figurines and animal slippers – not just in people, but in animals, too. I'm so relieved my Martha is okay."

"Is Speedy like you and me? Can he see and hear?"

"No, is Christaine?"

"No."

Chapter 15: FROM THE OLD ESTATE

I've been thinking about Nell – me, Aubrey. About her mom, and her mom's murder in 1954. It was the Tin Snip Killer. Nell was nine. Me, too. I heard her mom had slapped her in front of the bookstore Sonny owned. Everyone knew Sonny. Sonny told me he saw it happen. Said it wasn't right to hit a kid like that. He was abnormal and furious about it.

I remember when Nell flipped that day, years later, in the seventh grade. How the ambulance people carried her out of the classroom. How me, Punky, The Junior, and Arquette followed them to the street with the Ball jar she always brought to class, the one with a cricket inside she called Black Socks, the one she talked to and said it talked to her like Triple Suiter talks to me. The look on her face as they lifted her inside the ambulance still sitting in her school desk because she wouldn't let go. I can see the shitty extravaganza of it. I know now how that feels when the mess hall shows up, when you pass through a flank muscle with a bad passenger, a bad slipper. I have one I call the Slim Hand. I've been trying to put a fleabane between him and me for years. He takes me to a room through the flank when I lose it, a place where my pica, my compulsion to swallow a large object like a bathtub or toaster comes over me. Crazy, I know, what I can't help for God's sake. I hear him count, one Mississippi, two Mississippi… then red men put holes in my hands and hoist me to the top of the Blind Spot Cathedral, my arms stretched out like my old heroes, Christ Jesus, Vitruvian, and the Great or Lesser Morrison. That's where Nell went the day she flipped in class, to another mess hall, some blind spot in her head when repression failed her. I heard she had seen the picture the police had of her mother's body after they found it, all fetus like, curled in the Tin Snip's refrigerator. The fiend left the door open to see the red gashes he'd made in her, and red means run son. Run, and don't you limp, either.

Nell was in the Palm Beach Place of Rest for thirty-five years, her father a wealthy man. I would go to see her, but not enough, my conscience told me. I went, and Sonny from the bookstore went because he always liked Nell. No one else in our class did, but no one else had that thing with Nell like I had, a slipper in their head, and Nell and I had told each other we had one. We were kids. I was scraggly and pale, Nell was beautiful, my Jean Seberg from the movie *Lilith*. That's what I called her when I was nineteen and that film came out. Back then, there were so many movies in your life you hardly had time to be yourself. You were always in one. I couldn't believe it when I saw that film. I dropped my Coke. There was Nell, in *Lilith*, a movie star in the booby hatch like Seberg, all blond and perfect for me to get institutionalized over, too, because I was Warren Beatty. I went to see her in that crazy place even when I was married. I ached for her back then. But as my life became a distraction, I went less and less. Then she came back to town with a pass to live on her own. She showed up at my gate one morning and wanted to rent something for a studio to do her artwork. Christaine and I talked about it and rented her the guest house on the old property up the road. Christaine liked her right away and got close with her. Nell goes back to town at night to be with her sick father and the nursing staff. My crush is not the same. I love Christaine.

Aubrey

Chapter 16: FREDDIE TOMMIE

In 1987, Freddie married a thirty-two-year-old Seminole girl, a divorcee, and they had a child they named Yuchee Cowkeeper Tommie. Freddie did what he could to act normal, but his mind was full of ghosts and madness from the war, and that made him trying. The woman eventually divorced him. Freddie had every other weekend with his son. He was a hero to his boy, like Aubrey was to his. He came to Aubrey's place one Saturday morning and brought Yuchee. Aubrey came out on the porch when Freddie was halfway up the walk. Freddie seemed to feel funny about coming further until Aubrey asked if he wanted a coffee and was he going to drink it on the walk or come in the damn house.

"I haven't seen you in a long time," Aubrey said. "The Junior was still alive, and you showed up at The Blue Goose once. You didn't stay very long, and you didn't say much."

"Sorry I didn't make it to Junior's funeral. I was in Mexico at one of the old Black Seminole towns. I have a sister there."

"Well, we sent him off best we could in a cypress coffin with his boots on."

"Yeah, I knew The Junior could count on you for that, yes?"

"The whole thing kinda gutted me and everyone that knew him."

Freddie's son sat in a porch chair, silent.

"I came over, well, to say hello to you, and I heard you have a boy same age as my boy here," Freddie said.

"I do. He's at the store with his mother. Should be back soon."

Freddie looked over at his son and said, "Stand up, boy." The child stood and poked out his chest and chin. "This is Yuchee Tommie. I have him on weekends because his mother and I, well, you know. You say hello to Mr. Shallcross." Aubrey stuck out his hand and they shook.

"And where do you live, Yuchee?"

"Brighton. The reservation, sir."

"Ah, yes, out in the real good country west of the lake."

"Yes, sir."

A car pulled in. It was Nell on her way up the shell rock road to the other house, the house the old Blue Goose bunch called O'gram, after its parallelogram shape and slight reference to cocaine back then. Nell, barefoot blond in tie-dye clothes she made for herself. Her hair was in this kind of careless freedom below some piece of wild-ass-looking cloth hat, her skin so sunless that Freddie probably wondered if she had any blood. Looking at her Seberg face and figure, though, Freddie probably wasn't sure if he had any, either. Aubrey introduced her. Nell moved her lower lip to the left and chewed the inside twice like Aubrey did sometimes.

"You're a suitcase full of clothes. All kinds," she said to Freddie. "You're rare. So many of us in you. The French would call you a *portmanteau*. I knew I would see a good one, one day." Freddie frowned, unsure. "Aubrey," she said, "I just got this in the mail. It's from a lawyer. Would you look at it for me? I think it says I've been given some property, and from guess who."

"Give up."

"Sonny. You know, who had the little bookstore downtown." It made a noise in Aubrey's head when she said "downtown."

"Is he dead? I thought he was just missing or gone."

"Read it. It says he was declared dead. Anyway, you please read it. I don't understand all of it."

"Says here it's yours if you pay the back taxes."

Christaine pulled up with Drayton. The two little boys went off to play. Nell sat and drank coffee. Aubrey filled her in on Freddie and how he was in the war with The Junior. Freddie uncharacteristically carried on a fair conversation and then, even more uncharacteristically, asked if he could see the house up the road The Junior had told him so much about.

"Nell has a key. Follow her. Christaine and I will watch your boy. Go on up there and look around. Nell – she'll show you the place."

"Want another cup of coffee?" Nell asked when they got to the house and walked across the pool deck to her cottage. Freddie nodded, looking at the strange wooden land ship and its angular reaches.

"You drink a lot of coffee?" he asked.

"Yes. In the mornings I take too much medicine, so the coffee keeps me from getting the slows."

They sat at a small table. "Why medicine?"

"I spent a long time in a special place for crazies because I see and hear things, and for years I heard some bad things along with the good things. I called them the screaming poison people. Aubrey would come to see me, especially when his mother was dying of this long disease called Lou Gehrig's. He told me his mother was his hero, that he called her his 'steel hibiscus' instead of a steel magnolia, because she would sink a hibiscus attached to a lead weight in a big brandy snifter full of water and put it on the living room table. He said he had to make her into a hibiscus because this was South Florida, and not a lot of magnolias down here. He told me I had to be a steel hibiscus, too, while I was in the 'place,' he called it, so I could get out of there one day. So that's what I made me into, a hibiscus, and here I am."

"My friends say I need to take medicine," from Freddie.

"Do you?" she said, staring at his mixed blood lineaments she earlier referred to as a suitcase full of clothes.

"Yes, certain smoke from plants and special parts of animals instead of pills."

"Wish I was an Indian."

"Anybody can be, one way or another. It's being pure white that must be hard, yes?"

"*True* magazine," Nell said.

Freddie nodded and looked around the room. "I like your dolls in the cabinet there. But those two on the left are hard for me to understand."

Nell brought them to the table. "These are dolls I made of my friends from the so called Palm Beach Place of Rest when I was there. Real people I knew and hung out with. When I graduated, so to speak, I took the dolls with me so I would always remember them. My friends are still there. One girl, this doll on the left, was an anorexic. We all had nicknames in that place and hers was Air Plant, but I called her Orchid, because she was a beautiful air plant. You know, that's all they live on. This other doll was a boy I knew there."

"The one who's wearing a mask of some kind, like mosquito netting, yes?"

"Yes, it's called a spit mask. He couldn't control himself and would spit on people. He was considered, well…"

"He looks like a beekeeper with that on."

"Sometimes so much spit would accumulate on the inside of the mask he couldn't see, and they would have to clean it and put it back on him again. He never seemed to understand the spit wouldn't go through the mask. He just liked to spit, anyway, I think. No one wanted to get near him except me. He didn't go off the wall when I talked to him, and he told me once everyone around him except me told stethoscope lies, and he could hear their hearts beating children. His nickname was, you guessed it, Spit Mask."

"It was?"

"It was. And ever since he told me what he told me, I believe I can hear certain hearts when they are lying and beating children, too."

"Did you have a nickname?"

"Black Socks."

"You wore them, yes?"

"No, I have a sidecar. A slipper. Aubrey has one, too. He told me that's what we should call them. Slippers – they're like sidecars attached to a motorcycle. My sidecar's name is Black Socks because he's a cricket with black legs and black socks, you know. Sidecars and slippers are people that live in your head. You talk to them and they talk back. Nobody ever believes they're real besides you and others who have them. Aubrey's sidecar is called Triple Suiter. Aubrey and I knew about all this when we were nine years old and in the fourth grade together. We would talk about it alone so the other kids wouldn't think we were crazy. I went away soon after that. Don't tell Christaine about Aubrey's sidecar. Aubrey wants to be the one who does, although I think Christaine knows. She knows about my mine. I told her because she is very cool and knows a lot about most everything, I think. Her name means blood stain – Jesus Christ blood stain. You know. Everyone knows about me in this small town. I bet when I walk downtown, people say, 'There goes crazy Nell.' Do you have a sidecar, Freddie?"

Freddie stared at her for a second, his head kind of running from Nell's speed talk, then he looked at the floor, smiled the rare one, and said, "Yes."

"What's its name?"

"*Allapatta.*"

"You said that with an accent. Does it mean something in Indian?"

"Alligator. One day you should meet my friends like I met yours today. The dolls, I mean. You would like my *yaholi*."

"What's that?"

"A medicine man, you know, like in the movies, yes?"

"Don't put that on me. I'm not someone who measures Indians with the movies."

He stared more. Looked embarrassed. "I believe you're not that person, Nell. The *yaholi* is my advisor. His name is Billie Monday. He is Seminole, and he is from an ancient African man, his great-great-grandfather, who was called Uncle Monday, but most of the tribe believes he is the same person and lives in the water as an alligator when he is not around as a man. They think he comes out of the water for a while as a man to be with the tribe, and then goes back in to be an alligator again, yes? He saved me when I came home from the war. I was haunted by the people I killed. I was sure they were in the spirit world drawing pictures of me, and I was sure their families still living were drawing pictures of me in Vietnam and lighting them on fire. I feel bad about killing another warrior, but not about killing people who do not deserve to live, yes?"

Nell moved close enough to Freddie to make him nervous. "You promise you will take me to see him, your medicine man."

"I promise."

They went over to the empty main house. Freddie asked if he could be alone inside for a while. Nell said, "That's exactly what I wanted to do the first time I came here. It's a house of all movies. And oh, you have someone in your eye."

"I know. An *allapatta*," Freddie said and smiled. She left.

"Get a good look at the place?" Aubrey asked when he came back for his son.

"I don't know you well enough to say this, but I think I am right. It is a House of you. It is exactly you, yes?"

"Probably. Can we speak privately about the other House we've seen? The one that comes out of the water and the woods when I camp by the creek on the Zarnitz Ranch? You see, the members of that House have told me you know them, and that you and Billie Monday are helping them."

"I know they have told you. I am honored to belong to that House with you, Aubrey Shallcross. The Junior and I belonged to a House in the war. It was a different House, that House. Violent, crazy. This House we belong to now can be violent, but it is not senseless like the war. You leave the violence to me, Aubrey. I will do that."

"I will for now." Aubrey nodded.

"The Junior and I learned some things in Vietnam from an educated man named Suskin. He was attracted to the tigers in the jungle there. He called the tigers the 'terrible and the sublime,' yes? He said this English man, William Blake, told him what it all meant in his writing, and that this is always going on, this terrible and sublime, and it's going on now in these waters around here when the *allapattas* crawl out, beautiful in their power and skins. Most forget about the terrible part and what it can do. I have heard people say they are mad at their god, but they are really mad at nature. People say they want the jungle, but they don't want the terrible jungle; they only want the sublime. I wear this ring on my finger to remember Suskin, who was killed by a bullet and his body mostly eaten by a tiger in Vietnam before they found what was left of him. It seemed fitting, the tiger coming to eat him, I mean. Now he rides forever with the tiger he was so fascinated with. As you see, my ring is a tiger's head with a small diamond in his teeth. This is all new to you, isn't it, Aubrey? The animals with the spirits, yes?"

"Not exactly. I've always known when you put your hand on something *animale*, it provides relief from being alone. I thought there might be something else in there. The fact that I can see and hear them now, these slippers the animals carry with them, yes, that part is new. I wear a ring, too, made from the brain stone of a giant toad. It changes colors, which mean different things."

"We understand the same things then. I talked close with Nell. She told me about her slipper and yours, and she told me about sidecars. I come from a religion that has always believed this."

Aubrey nodded. "Side cars. You and Nell did have a long talk."

"But of course, no mention to her of this new House you and I belong to in the jungle, the one from the Breath Master, yes?"

"I *do* have a side car, Freddie, a slipper. One I talk to all the time and him to me. I always thought horses and dogs were full of these same spirits. In fact, all my life, I could never tell them apart sometimes, animals and people. Will you let me know when it's time for me to help the House?"

"I will. But they could send the gypsy with the snake to tell you before I do." They locked eyes for a few seconds.

Aubrey took Freddie to say goodbye to Christaine. Drayton and Yuchee were upstairs. They walked up to Drayton's room and the boys were on the floor riding the eight-foot stuffed alligator. Freddie's eyes opened wide when he saw them, and he started laughing.

"I got Henry, the taxidermy guy out in Indiantown, to do this for me. Do you know him?"

"I know him," Freddie answered. "I would go over there when The Junior was still alive. Henry asked me to help him with something a year ago, and I have been going over there lately more and more this year."

"What was it he wanted help with?"

"I thought you might know. Anyway, maybe we meet at his house soon. He is doing things that interest me and I think would interest you, yes?"

"Come back any time, Freddie, and bring Yuchee. I have no one to talk close with about The Junior, and I'd like to talk about him and a lot of other things with you."

"Thank you."

Aubrey walked back to the house from Freddie's truck thinking about all that had been said – the connection he and Freddie shared with the past, and now the animal slippers. Just incredible this thing, this un-world that wasn't there weeks ago and now was. He would love to run this by the monks that schooled him in college. They'd work out a religious explanation, he bet. *What is the real difference between me now and the way I was when I was a Catholic?* he thought. He was still bitter about his old church, his ex-church that divorced its elegant wife and ran off with a younger woman. They dropped the Latin, they dropped the ball, they etiolated the rituals. The younger woman remodeled the church and turned the tacky new altars around to face the people. A lot of the church's old friends left after that syrupy holding hands and other modern dreck showed up. *When I was Christian, we were told we were half-human half-divine, because we had been given a soul. Now I'm an atheist, and I'm still half-human and half-divine, like Nemo and Osceola. I'd love to take the monks to my campsite by the creek to meet these half-breeds that have nothing to do with their church.*

On the porch, he still heard the echoes of his son and Freddie's running around the yard while Freddie was up at the other house with Nell. *And what is this with Nell inheriting a place from ole Sonny? She said he was declared dead.*

Chapter 17: VISIT TO HENRY'S

Aubrey takes Drayton and Christaine to the carnival's winter quarters one morning to watch Speedy practice inside the Globe of Death. They all sit under a banyan, drink coffee, and eat the pastries Roberta made.

Speedy started with a careful rock back and forth inside the spherical cage, then stopped to adjust when he heard something in the bike he didn't like. Began again, rocking up the wall and back down, higher and higher, until he chanced a complete revolution upside down, followed by many more. Drayton was run through by it.

At the table under the banyan, Speedy explained the new stuff he was trying to work out with the bike – the intricacies of timing. Beyond the banyan, part of another high cage could be seen with a canvas floor. It was empty. Aubrey wanted to know what it was and wanted to walk back there. Speedy looked at Roberta and Roberta's return look was, no. Aubrey wanted to know what was going on when he saw that look. He kidded them and laughed. "Ah, ah. I have discovered some great carnival secret only those with the show are allowed."

"It isn't that it is such a secret; it's just if Vito sees you looking around his equipment, he'll make a scene. He has many times before," Roberta said.

"What if I trade you one of my secrets for one of yours on the show?"

"Roberta, tell him. We know him. It's okay. Besides, lots of local men know what goes on over there," claimed Speedy.

"Yes, but the real problem is ours, Speedy. Vito is going to get us all in trouble, especially acts like mine with animals, and that is the real *not*-so-secret. I could lose my snake act because of him."

"Tell me the secret and I'll trade you one of mine," Aubrey said. "And you're going to like it, Roberta. I'll just say one word. *Snake.*"

"Tell him the whole story, Roberta. Aubrey and Christaine are our friends. He even wants to trade you one."

Roberta said Vito had a chimpanzee act and was also part owner of the main show. He was always just an inch away from the Humane Society. Often, he had to fix the sheriff's favorite charity to run his act in a new town. Vito put on a late show with a full-grown male chimp, a big one called Kong – hard to handle. One he kept out of sight. The spectacle was a prize fight inside the big cage. Any man with a hundred dollars was invited to try to go two minutes with the gloved and muzzled chimp; the pay-  off was a thousand dollars if he lasted. No one usually lasted more than thirty seconds before the chimp kicked them to the floor. The chimp always had two handlers with ropes attached to each side of his collar and muzzle, even during the fight. After it was over, they would pull him off his human opponent.

Roberta said in the old days, when she was a child travelling with her show folks, she saw this kind of stuff all the time. Not so much anymore. It was amazing, she said, that Vito could get away with it in this day and age. Everyone on the show disliked him because he had a mean stripe and was a druggie and a drunk.

"Okay. That's the secret here. Now you owe me one, Aubrey."

Everyone at the table laughed.

"This is a story that can only be shown, not told," Aubrey said, "and only after I talk the man at the center into letting you see."

"You're not stalling, are you? Is it really about snakes?"

"Yes, but give me two days. I promise it'll be worth it if this man will go along, and I'm pretty sure he will."

"Two days then." Roberta hard-eyed and soft-smiled him.

"I get to go, too," Speedy said.

"Sure, and there's much more than the snakes. There's the most outrageous house of taxidermy you've ever seen, and the guy himself does all the mounts. We call him the Tax Man."

When Aubrey called the "Tax Man" Henry, it took some humble jawing to get him to visit with his new friends. At first, Henry knocked him for not staying in touch. Aubrey reminded him he had been shot, and the last two years had been rearranging his life. He knew it was going to take more than a phone call. There was only one Henry, the master of preservation, a backwoods weirdo who was a good story in itself, one to certainly get even with Roberta. Aubrey told him to meet at the Johnny Jumper Inn tomorrow in Indiantown, twenty miles west of the coast, and he would give him the background on Roberta and Speedy. He bet Henry would cave like a two-dollar suitcase once he knew about them and their acts.

The next night, they sat. Aubrey immediately put Henry in the way of a promotional photo of Roberta and Speedy.

"You mean to tell me this woman has no legs at all?" Henry said.

"That's right, boyeh. And she can handle a coach whip, the meanest snake on the ground, as you well know. I've seen it!"

"Can I look at her naked?"

"Uh, no. That guy with the big arms in the photo here is

her husband, the one that rides motorcycles upside down in a Motordrome, so I don't think…"

"What if I pay for it? They carnie people, ain't they?"

"Yeah, Henry, but proud carnies."

Henry yelled towards the bar, "Hey, Cabbage, come 'ere, man, and bring us two more shots of that shark snot."

"What? Holy shit," Cabbage the bartender hollered, looking at the photo of Roberta, snakes coiled all around her, and Speedy sitting on one of his motorcycles.

"Yeah, how would you like to meet them, boyeh? Aubrey's bringin 'em out to my place this week."

It was all set. Three days later, the group drove out to Henry's. Christaine wasn't that interested. She knew what was there, and she had a thing about the taxidermy Henry was doing. She told Aubrey no way Drayton was going, either. Too dangerous. "God knows what that swamp rat is up to." In the meantime, Aubrey sent word to Freddie Tommie he would be there.

At the gate, same drill from the old days – call the house a hundred yards up the driveway on the intercom so Henry could decide whether to let you in.

"Who's that?"

"Head Wound, Tax Man."

"Jesus, son. Like I said the other night, thought you mighta forgot who I was."

"That's what I mean, oh, great resurrectionist. I mean, I just remembered myself. Shot in the head. Remember, fucker?"

"Very funny, Shallcross." Henry's gate made an electric noise and swung open. Up to the house, and in the yard stood Henry and Freddie Tommie.

"Henry, this is Roberta and Speedy. They are with the carnival that winters on the South Fork next to town. And by God, there's Freddie."

Henry nodded and tried not to stare at Speedy carrying Roberta in his arms.

"And you know this indigenous renegade Freddie Tommie," Henry said, "who was in 'Nam with The Junior."

"Yes, I do. Freddie, Roberta and Speedy."

"Well, hell. Let's go in the house. I got beer and beer if you want one. Don't have much else."

They all sat on the sofa around the famous wagon wheel table, the one that turned like a lazy Susan and freighted lines of coke around to all the cowboys and shit kickers in the old days at Henry's parties. They were surrounded by piece after amazing piece of taxidermy. Henry asked a lot of questions about Roberta's snake act and wanted to know the particulars of training a coach whip because he thought it impossible. Roberta indulged him as best she could without getting too much into the paranormal she was blessed with. Henry must have looked to her like he couldn't take that.

"Yeah, I been interested in reptiles ever since I was kid," Henry told her. "Had me a pet horned lizard my uncle brought me from Arizona. That thing could puff up like a chuckwalla when he was scared. But the best part is that they fill their eyelids full of blood, then squirt it out six feet through their tear ducts at somethin to scare the hell outta them."

"Ah, yes, I know about them. I had a hognose snake when I was a little girl, and it would play dead if it was frightened. The best part was that it would even hang its tongue out of its mouth like it was truly dead. Now where in the world do you think they learned to do that?"

Henry looked at Roberta almost affectionately.

There was another a feeling in the room. It was in this room where The Junior's death trip started six years ago: He danced around at a party holding one of Henry's future mounts, a live coral snake, sticking out his tongue at the colorful head until it struck and bit him in the tongue. The story was told in its entirety to the others, and Roberta was beyond belief at the chances of that. Freddie sat quiet. He put his hands over his face eventually, and when he took them down it was tear-streaked. Aubrey told him it must have seemed like an ignoble death after all they went through in Vietnam, and Freddie said no, in his world, this was a very noble way to die, to have sacred poison from a snake bring you a powerful last dream.

"All right. All right," Henry said. "I got something out back I wanna show y'all, if you can keep a secret. Nothing personal, you new friends, but if you weren't with Aubrey Shallcross, no way I let you see it."

On the way, Henry showed Speedy his old dirt bikes in a shed, so old they were Harley Davidson dirt bikes, a one-time folly by the Harley people in the 70s to get into the market, but they quit after a couple of years and stuck to their street machines.

"Come on while I feed up my farm."

A six-foot-high concrete block wall encircled an area. "Must have cost some money to build this," Aubrey said.

"So what? Come on, Shallcross. What I got in here will jar your memory, Florida boy."

They walked through the solid gate and didn't see anything but pine trees and scrub palmettos at first, until they heard a sound they all knew right away – rattles, many, singing from diamond backs all over the ground. Henry laughed at the first snake. Stuck his leg out towards it. When it struck it made a thumping noise on Henry's leg. The poison ran down his jeans. Henry winked, and pulled up his pant leg to show them the thin aluminum snake bite boot he was wearing.

"I'm farmin 'em, by God."

"You're what?" Aubrey said, backing up with Speedy, who was holding Roberta higher in his arms.

"Yep. There ain't so many of 'em left anymore like there was when we was kids, cause the bulldozers and housing developments killed or run 'em off. Now the woods is run over with damn rats and vermin; they even gnawing on my taxidermy in the warehouse. I'm gonna repopulate the state with these old crawling crackers, balance things up, if that's what it takes."

"You're what?"

"*True* fuckin magazine, Shallcross. And over there in them palmettos is where the female snakes have all the babies. And let me show you my other project." They walked to an area where two high wire cages were – aviaries holding a half-dozen small gray hawks with piercing red eyes and long talons.

"On top of the rattlesnake thing, I got this crazy idea I could train these here Everglades snail kites that are losing their food source. I'm teachin 'em to eat more than apple snails. I'm gonna teach 'em to eat baby snakes."

"Rattlesnakes?"

"No, son, them damn python babies taking over the 'Glades out there. Look over here in this shed. This is where I hatch out the little pythons so I can feed 'em to the snail kites. They raise them pythons by the hundreds down in Homestead, and my ex brother-in-law works in one of them rebuilt pet farms after Hurricane Andrew blew up the place. Sneaks real python eggs for me."

Aubrey turned to Speedy and Roberta. "How do you like my secret so far?"

"You win the secret contest," Roberta said.

"You see," Henry continued, "they got these damn foreign snails taking over the 'Glades. They got such a different curl to their shell, and the 'Glades kites can't get that beak of theirs inside it to get the thing out, not like they can the native snails. So I'm gonna try it. Try to train 'em to eat something else. May not succeed, but I'll give it hell anyway, right, Shallcross?"

"Right, Tax Man. One question. How did you think up the kite thing?"

"Well, I got the idea drinkin one night, staring at the flag of Mexico in a bar. There's an eagle on that flag with a big rattlesnake in its mouth. I thought shit, bet I could train some kinda raptor round here to do that with them pythons. Maybe get the state to pay me."

"Yeah but how did you get the birds?"

"Freddie and his friend Billie Monday, that spooky old medicine man, know how to find 'em, climb up, and get the eggs and chicks."

Not long after this, Henry and Freddie starting riding around in Henry's truck, dropping baby rattlesnakes in areas that looked good for habitat; even areas that ran up close to the edge of housing developments and shopping centers. "I don' care if one of their kids get bit," Henry told Freddie. "Hell, let 'em have a little adventure in their life, like we did growing up. They can learn to watch where they put their damn feet in the woods like we had to, 'cause we knew Jake was everywhere, like he fuckin oughta be. They probably ain't gonna die from a bite. They might scream in the hospital and see Jesus for a couple days, but that'll build some character in them soft-boiled brats. My old man tol' me once that inside a rattler's rattles there's a dust, and if you get it in your eyes, it'll blind ya. Course, it ain't true. He did that to scare me, so I'd be lookin for 'em when I was walking through the woods. Right, Freddie, man?"

Occasionally they stopped the truck so Freddie could run up to a Brazilian pepper patch along the road and spread a few lethal crane droppings to kill the invader trees choking the ditch banks.

"We come back in a year, Henry, those trees will all be dead, yes?"

"I gotta see that shit, Freddie."

When Henry thought his snail kites were ready, he and Freddie drove to the Loxahatchee Wildlife Area at the north end of the 'Glades. They sat in the truck and waited with their binoculars after releasing three of the young birds.

"Shit, if those little fuckers show up on a branch with snails in their mouths instead of baby snakes, I'm gonna cut my skinny wrists. Not supposed to even know what a snail is after the way I raised 'em."

They saw the kites circling the hammocks out in the marsh. The birds started circling the truck, too, now and then, hoping Henry would feed them. He told Freddie, "They're damn hungry. I starved 'em pretty good before I brought 'em out here."

They had to move further down the berm to different spots occasionally for visual contact with the birds and to convince the hawks they had to hunt on their own. It was spring, the dry season, so the ground exposure had increased, and if there were any python babies, this was the time of year. It would take a hawk to see them; most men didn't, even when looking right at them.

"What if they get a rattlesnake or moccasin baby instead?" Freddie asked.

"C'mon, Freddie, man. It's too damn wet, even in the dry season, out there, and them moccasins are all black and under the lower water practically. Don't look nothin like a baby python, anyway."

Freddie nodded, then, kerplooee! Henry saw one had a small snake.

"A python, yes?" Freddie asked.

"Yeehaw! Don't ruin it for me, Freddie. I can't tell from here, but at least that fucker got a baby snake." Henry was jumping up and down in the truck seat.

~

Aubrey was still thinking about the fight cage he saw at the show grounds and the story Roberta told him about Vito and the big chimp.

The carnival was open for the county fair again this week, and the Shallcross family went, including the grandparents, Asante and Solana. After Drayton dragged them from game table to counter trying to win a teddy bear, Aubrey finally won throwing baseballs at milk bottles and gave Drayton the bear so he'd shut up about it.

They finished the evening with Roberta's snake act and Speedy's Globe of Death.

Christaine, Drayton, and her folks were tired and went home. Aubrey stayed for the midnight show behind the show, the one that pitched the ape against someone from the audience. He met Speedy at his trailer and they had a drink, then took a seat for the fight on benches in front of the big cage. Trip Suiter was so excited in Aubrey's head, he decided to narrate the whole scene as it was happening to his own slipper, Amper Sand, the world-class typist.

Vito came out with a microphone and laid out the proposition: "Any man who can last for two minutes with the ape will win a thousand dollars. You are allowed two falls. After the third fall, you are eliminated."

They brought out the jungle fighter. He was extra big for a mature chimp, five feet tall, wearing a muzzle collar with rings attached to each side. A rope through each of the rings had a handler at the end. The chimpanzee was dressed in burgundy boxer shorts, like a human fighter, with custom boxing gloves. On his feet were black and white Chuck Taylor's, embarrassing accessories, an embarrassment Aubrey thought he could see in the chimp's face.

Vito claimed it was not hard to beat the chimp and get a thousand dollars in your wallet. The first man volunteered from the audience, and Speedy violated show folk rules by whispering to Aubrey the man was a shill, a setup. The ape knew him and played with him every other day for food. Speedy said the chimp liked this man because he fed him, but the chimp was terrified of strangers. He also told Aubrey that Vito had the guys who worked the carnival rides poke and tease the chimp, while the regular handlers held him back, to keep him mean. Speedy said the chimp was super strong, like all of his kind, and would tear a man apart, even someone he knew if he got mad enough, without the ropes from the handlers.

The bell rang and they circled. The setup man from the show moved in. The handlers circled with them and watched, holding the ropes with just enough slack so the chimp could fight. There was a grab, a grip, a release, another grab with a lock around each fighter's neck, and they spun until the man released. The man grabbed on again and lifted the chimp off his feet; they both went to the floor. It had the look of someone playing with their dog. The chimp struggled loose and jumped up, then approached, kicked the man in the midsection, and landed two light punches. The man went down and got back up. That was one fall each. Time was on a clock above the ring; there were one and a half minutes left. The two fighters stood back and recovered themselves.

The crowd was up about it now. They thought the man was going to make it to the bell. With a minute to go, the man and the chimp locked on again, both fell down together, separated, and were quickly on their feet. The score was two falls each now. Through the muzzle, Aubrey saw the chimp raise his upper lip in a smile. With fifteen seconds left, the chimp kicked and pounded the man, who feigned a head and body move and grabbed the chimp by one leg and took him to the floor. The handlers separated them.

"Oh!" Vito yells, "He did it! He did it! It was a clear knockdown for the third time."

The man acted wobbly and kept shaking his head. Vito pulled a wad from his pocket and counted out ten one hundred dollar bills, making a big deal out of it of course. The man was helped out of the ring with the crowd cheering, and he held up the money he had won. A woman came up – she played his wife, Speedy said – and shook her finger at him. They left together and disappeared out on the midway.

"C'mon. Who wants to try to beat the great Kong? Get him while he's tired after that fight."

Another man stepped up – stacked, wide, rounded shoulders under a big head.

"Go get 'em, Sandy. Put it on him, Sandy," a crowd member yells. The man counted one hundred dollars out to fight the ape.

In the first five seconds they circled each other, the chimp swaying a little as he walked sideways. The handlers left more slack in the rope this time to give him some freedom. The man took a swing and hit the chimp in the head. The chimp kept walking sideways until he leapt in the air and came down on the man's head with both arms encircling his neck and kicked him twice in the gut. The man flew back against the cage. The handlers pulled the chimp off to let the man recover. He looked surprised. He assumed the position again, leading with his left foot to hold back his right shoulder for a gun-shot punch. They charged each other. Then the ape from Africa, the same place we are all from, flew into a flurry of fists and kicks that floored Joe Human, and Joe did not get up. The handlers dragged the chimp to the corner of the cage, and Aubrey saw the rage in his face and eyes. Once in the corner, Kong screamed, the same screams we scream.

"I gotta get going," he said to Speedy. "I just wanted to see what went on."

They walked to the center of the show grounds so Aubrey could say goodnight to Roberta.

On the way home, Aubrey asked, "Trip, did you see all that?"

"Not only did I see it, I narrated the whole scene for Amper Sand, who typed it like an insane. I described every second of the action. He doesn't get to see it through your eyes sometimes like I do, so I fill him in on things."

"Kinda leaves you a little sick watching what Vito is doing with that cousin, dressing him up like a buffoon and making him fight."

"Vito will pay for that one day."

"Wonder if Kong has a slipper?"

"Probably. If he does, Vito's in trouble."

Chapter 18: THE SHELL ROCK ROAD

The child grew inside the mockingbird egg Aubrey saw in his mind after he went limp with Christaine on the living room floor five years ago. Now Drayton sat on the front seat of his daddy's truck, another unknown soldier with original sin.

"God never making anything without a crack in it," Aubrey's grandmother would say. Aubrey wondered if he was seeing an actual conception that night he made love to Christaine – the beginning of this child, his child, her child, world child.

They drove up the shell road to the old house. Two years ago, Carlos tortured Aubrey and Christaine in the upstairs bedroom. Drayton was only two at the time. Carlos locked him in a closet and in the end, shot Aubrey. Too many griffins for Christaine to live there now, and Aubrey didn't blame her, but he'd either been able to shelve it or the bullet destroyed an area of garbage can in his memory. He didn't fear things as much since the bullet, and it made him slightly unconscionable about stuff that used to bother him.

In the living room, the enshrined dioramas of taxidermy stood along the walls – mannequins and murals behind Plexiglass, the real and imagined Plexiglass he once used as a mental image to protect him when he was younger, and now he felt he didn't need it. Maybe that was the bullet again.

He went upstairs and stood at the end of the wide bed from his past. In the center of the headboard was the neon sign that said FLORIST. He was crazy about neon back then, but he'd smashed the colored tube piece of Leda and the Swan on the wall downstairs right after his young wife left.

Hidden in the bathroom wall was the hand-hammered chalice that held the toadstone ring. Reve, the old Gypsy woman that lived on the river, had made the ring for him when he turned thirteen. It had been his coming of age present two days before the bishop of the diocese slapped his face at his confirmation. And though his father and grandmother made a big deal out of the Catholic ritual, he much preferred the *crapudine* ring on the river bank that night; who else had a ring made from the brain stone of a pagan toad? He put it on. Thought he was going to need its forecast since he had recently joined the supernatural house of sagacious slippers by the creek. It made him think about his grandmother. She loved him so. When he was ten years old, he overheard her telling the neighbor lady, "You know, Aubrey never stops talking, and he can go on about invisible creatures and pirates and things. I think he really believes it. I do hope our Lord doesn't consider that lying."

On the top deck of the house, he looked out across his land. "Is this my empire?" he said to the woods. "No. I am my empire. My head is my mansion."

"Aubrey," Trip said to him, "quit fingering the finery. Where is your boy? You walked off and left him downstairs like a blond person."

Drayton was at the bottom of the ladder. "Daddy!"

"No, no, don't come up. I'll come down to you. Do you remember being in this room when you were a baby boy?"

The child nodded, but did he really remember when he was locked in the closet? Dead now, that animal Carlos. Aubrey hoped Drayton remembered nothing from that night. The child had said nothing to them, so maybe it was true.

Drayton saw the ring on his father's hand and touched it. Aubrey told him about it changing colors and that the colors meant different things. He told him the power of the ring. Drayton's eyes quit blinking.

They walked across the pool deck to say hello to Nell, but she wasn't there, even though her car was. *On one of her walks*, he thought.

When he was driving across the wetland on the road, back to the other house, he stopped for a minute. "This is a place I call the knee-high Serengeti," he said, pointing to the marsh. "See the small plants in the water? They look like the little acacia trees on the Serengeti plain in Africa. This is where Daddy used to fly his airplane."

"Where is the airplane?" his boy said.

"Right here. Right here in the tabernacle of my truck. This is my airplane." He banged on the steering wheel. "This toadstone ring on my finger turns my truck into an airplane when I want it to."

"Un-uh!" Drayton shook his head. "This is a truck. What's a tabinackle?"

"A sacred place. The cab of a man's truck is a sacred place. A holy place, like a church. So it's a kind of tabernacle."

"Like Grandma and Grandpa's church?"

"Yeah, like when they take you to St. Joseph's. That's a tabernacle, a sanctuary, a church. Wanna fly my truck?" Aubrey made airplane sounds and rubbed the toadstone ring, while the child laughed and made the sounds with him.

"Here we go in our flying truck! We're up in the air, making a turn to the left and then to the right. Now we're in a dive, and we level off out over the savannah below and just glide, no engine, so quiet. Aw, look at it down there, Drayton. It's beautiful."

Drayton let out a little boy scream and more airplane sounds. Tiny gleets flew out of his mouth from the sputtering.

"Now we're going to land back on the shell rock road. We glide and glide, then bounce, bounce, and we are here again and come to a stop on the air strip, emerging swollen and exhilarated. Can you carburet that, kid?"

"I glide, too, Daddy. Mommy calls it a daydream, but I call it a glider, my daydreams."

"Me, too. I daydream. I drift, like a boat. So I call it a drifty."

"And you talk to your slipper, don't you, Daddy? I got a slipper, too."

"Oh, yeah? What's his name?"

"Tree Frog."

Aubrey cracked up. "Tree Frog! Good one."

He sat there for a minute. Drayton turned his attention to a flashlight he was fooling with. Out in the wetland, Aubrey saw it all again. He went to the back peal of his life and moved things around. So much dream punk in his time had been performed on this shell rock road, so many wonderful drifties. The morning spider webs he had turned into stories, the bucking horses he rode high as hooked sailfish, the cattle drives he and The Junior worked, the comical fights they got into with people in bars. He saw Reve, the wise old woman. She taught him to believe in magic and visions – the good people on crosses out in the wetlands after he was shot – the grand returns from this unusual life he had led, his love for Christaine, the dome in his head where the cane field and tower he built let him conjure anything he wanted on the right day.

And the dark stuff he saw too: The banana mangoes in his hands he would bring his dying mother, the fear of the red hourglass he'd seen on the black widow's stomach, the rattlesnake that swallowed a squirrel and crawled inside his head to a gallery of x-rays – picture after picture of human chests with squirrels stuck in throats, like breech babies that caused his pica to come that day.

The choke. He was convinced he had swallowed the rattlesnake, the squirrel, and all the x-rays. The snake spoke to him in Reve's voice, telling him it was the sand skink and the flame vine blooming in the yards around town that made these bad things land on him – his pica, his mother's death, Carlos, the inevitable errors in a life. He began to cry. Drayton saw it, sitting there in the truck, but didn't say anything. Aubrey switched back and straightened out, wiped his eyes, and drove home.

He felt something was happening, something close. He felt this way years ago when Carlos was coming for Christaine, before he could ever know. What was it after these last weeks, these animal visions by the creek that weren't visions at all? If only Reve was alive to tell him, or someone like her that knew these things when they were coming. He had a feeling now that this person was Roberta from the carnival. Was she like Reve? Premonitions? Roberta knew about slippers and animals. With the Blue Goose bunch from the old days gone, a new bunch was forming. People had come home – Nell Kitching – or just showed up, like Freddie Tommie, Roberta, Speedy, and the slippers by the creek. Soon, Leda and his old friend Arquette would find him again.

That night, he dreamed. He was tiny, a slipper, walking around a lake to a strange black dock. On the dock, he felt it move. At the end was a small guard house with two glass doors. Through one of the doors came Nemo, his hand out with the palm up.

"Aubrey, come with me. I want to show you the underwater."

The glass doors were not doors, but the big eyes of The Dragon. The black dock was not a dock, but The Dragon's long tiled back. Inside the eyes, Nemo and Aubrey sat drinking wine, looking out at the water from a commodious room with a fireplace that talked to itself as it burned. Nemo told him stories about sinking war ships and travelling under the oceans a century ago in the Nautilus.

The Dragon left the shallow bank, folded his legs back against his body, and swam out to deeper water. Nemo gave the command "Dive," and the creature went down along the sand bottom over stretches of grass beds, his huge tail moving back and forth, sliding them around lily pad farms and sunken logs. Brim, blue gill, bass, shiners, turtles all watched – some moving, some still – their shadows staining the bottom. A big gar hit a blue gill and streaked the water red with blood and scales. The gator kept moving.

"There is a place ahead around this turn," Nemo said. "When I stop there, two children come out of the sand bottom, a brother and sister. They always sing to me and then go back into the sand where they live. Oh, look! There they are."

The Dragon stopped. The two figures swam up to The Dragon's eyes, just as Nemo said. They were dressed in clothes from the 1950s, and one, Harold, had his hair slicked back in duck's ass comb like Elvis. The girl swam closer.

"Hello, Aubrey. It's Betty and my brother Harold from the seventh grade. Remember? We drowned off Ski Point in 1957."

Aubrey stiffened, didn't blink. He made himself speak. "My Lord. I watched them drag the river for your bodies that day. Nell Kitching and I were at Ski Point. We were twelve years old, like you. You were still holding on to each other when they found you."

"Oh, yes. We left those bodies after we drowned and headed towards the clear water out by the St. Lucie Inlet."

"Did it hurt? The drowning, I mean."

"Ha! A delicious agony, right, Harold?"

Harold nodded and said, "We love it here."

"Sing us a song, mademoiselle," Nemo said.

The two moved closer.

"SLEEPY FISH, I CRAVE YOUR WATER

CRAVE YOUR LAND OF STIFLED TONES,

CRAVE THE DARKNESS YOU CAN HIDE IN,

HATE THE DAYLIGHT I HAVE KNOWN.

YOU CAN TUMBLE THROUGH YOUR OWN SKIES,

THEY GAVE ME THE GROUND FOR HOME,

BUT I TUMBLE, WHEN I FEEL HIGH,

TILL THE WATER TURNS TO FOAM.

HERE COMES THE MAN IN THE FLYING MACHINE,

THE AIR IS DIRTY, BUT THE WATER IS CLEAN."

"Hee, hee, hee, hee." The brother and sister swam away into the bottom, disappearing like flounder in the sand.

"It is what I call a *trompe l'oeil*, these two. It fools the eye," Nemo said.

Aubrey woke up.

Chapter 19: THE BEACH: JOHN CHROME

John Chrome, the beloved hip school teacher, surfer, and vocabular clown, is sitting with Aubrey at the Blue Goose.

"It's all in the King James manual," Chrome said. "I had this theory once. God and Satan split everything up after the contrarieties surfaced and settled it with prejudice, so they could keep going back to ask for child support, infinitely. But from whom? Whom do *they* answer to? Morrison? Elvis? The Indigo, Jesus? They – God, Satan – love that word infinity; rolls right off their tongues. They don't know what it means, just like us.

If they really knew what it meant, they would have moved on to something else by now, but they just keep dropping that word. The *mono* deities act so childish. So do the quantity Greek divines. And here we are, created in their image and likeness. Oh, goody."

"What do you mean you had this theory once? That God/Satan divorce thing is everyone's theory. What's your *new* theory?"

"Well, if I may perorate again, and with you, Shallcross, I can use the good stuff, because those Benedictines had you for years. You see, I believe the God of Abraham is not omnipotent and never was; he just had the Jews, Christians, and Mohammeds convinced he was. Satan and God have been pretty unevenly matched forever with the good and evil stuff; even in *Star Wars*, they're still working it, and God is losing. Even in *Star Wars*, nothing gets solved. In my classroom at the high school, I have to use pabulum like *Star Wars* as an example when the overly idealistic kids come on so 'change the world this time around, bro,' doo lang, doo lang. Fucking *Star Wars*, of all things, because these children won't sit still for *Don Quixote* or Spinoza, other than the book flaps and crib sheets they cop and mop at the library and book store.

"At least I tell the truth and somehow still keep my job, not like some of those other *manqué* motherfuckers on the board I teach with. Oh, but there will never be peace in the heavens; God and Satan are just, like that song says, 'slobs like one of us.' Taters, you like to call them, Shallcross – self-exal-taters. Blind ones that don't know they do it and sight ones that know they do, and I'm thinking God might be a blind tater, and Satan is definitely a sight tater. Satan knows he's a ball walker and will flounce to get your attention. He likes having a character flaw like that. He is Mister Character Flaw; he's Satan. But the God guy, the pavonine, the not-so-plain peacock, yet slob, doesn't know it, I tell you. He's a blind tater that wants to turn us all into talk walkers, stereotypes of him, that ole 'image and likeness' line from Genesis again. Shit, I miss our conversations, man."

Aubrey chewed the inside of his cheek flesh. "Hey, John, you know those two guys making a living off atheism in England? Dawkins and a writer named Hitchens? They're always bitching about how unjust this God is because he allows humans to starve to death; therefore, he must not exist. I wonder, though, is that the welfare theory working again, the one that says if you take handouts from the Hand, you lose respect for the Hand, like you would the government? The government's the Hand. Some good things at some time must have happened to those two English, something that makes them think they're either lucky or that there could be a nice God around. I think they want a candy-store God, one that should be taking better care of them. People usually end up despising the government for taking care of them, and now Dawkins and Hitchens despise God, the one they say doesn't exist and yet is doing a poor job."

"Like I said, I miss talking to you, man. C'mon, Aubrey, think we oughta do a little acid again?"

"MDA, I could do that again. I'm not supposed to do acid with this plate in my head. Probably MDA, too, but…"

"Sure. Right, might dissolve the thing," Chrome mumbled.

"Where's the clean stuff anymore?

"Same guy in Denver. I know one of his that gets it."

"What about that new drug the kiddies are doing that's similar – MMDA?"

"It's very different. They call it ecstasy or molly. It's more of a love-in, dance till you puke effect than a probing analytical rush like you get from the original MDA we used to do."

Chrome had the drug in a week. Aubrey talked with Christaine about it; said he was thinking about doing it again because it was so different from acid and not spooky. "Go ahead," she said, "but you have a child. So break one in half, Head Wound. I'm not raising him alone if you hit the wall."

They picked the day based on weather and the surf report, as usual. "Let's go down the beach to the Australian pines, same place." They had a cooler, a small boom box, beer, water, cold yogurt, fresh dark bread, and shade from the pines for when they took off.

They surfed. Chrome, his corpulent body doing 360s on the board, still the unlikely Bishop of the Beach, as he was for years in this town. Even if he didn't look athletic, he was king on a hydrol wall, carving and flipping the knife over the backside when he ran out of wave.

Up in the pines they dropped the drug; did the mandatory wait, no talking rule, though the pulse from the psychedelic amphetamine made you want to talk. This was the hard part, waiting for their blood levels to tell them it was time to lie down, watch the sky beyond the shade, and see the big change in clouds every time they opened and closed their eyes, thinking only two seconds had passed instead of three minutes.

"Now we can talk," Chrome said after an hour. "The good thing about this drug is you can you can get the words out. Not like acid, more of a speechless carburetion. Acid puts you where there are no words, where no words ever were, and those assholes that think they can describe that kind of place, well. I like my acid time, true, but when I want to talk, I like this drug, so let's get down like we used to and cover our old cryptonyms."

"Okay. Tell me about what you used to call the 'critical flicker,'" Aubrey said.

"You mean the luteous green light that comes when I see the chloroform candles in my head?"

"Yeah, that one, and tell me again about your vacuum state, the nothingness place. The 'wawa,' you call it. Like those Seven-Eleven-style stores up in Pennsylvania called WaWa, after that Indian tribe. Imagine meeting another Indian with a regal name like Apache and having to tell them you're a WaWa. Sounds like fucking baby talk."

"Yeah, right. It still goes on, my old stuff. Still have all that furniture. How about your designs? What's going on in your Mess Hall lately, Head Wound?"

"Let's see. I was on the road the other day. I pulled over to do some kind of neuromodulation that jumped me when my whittle monster got loose. When I was finished with that, I put my seat back to listen to the CB, then I heard it – a Jake brake. I mean, I've heard a million of them when the big trucks back off the pedal before an exit and it makes that budadaddda sound, coasting down on the engine's back pressure to slow the rig. Anyway, it occurred to me that sound was just like the 'wawa,' the cavitating outboard motor propellers make in air pockets when they rock back and forth in a boat wake, that sound, that dead zone sound, right? With acid, the dead zone doesn't have a sound, but with this drug it does, and even straight time without it does once you've heard it. Finished."

"You nailed it. Jake brake, huh. I buy that. It's fungible."

"Fungible?"

"Yeah, means interchangeable. I bet I can stick the Jake brake sound in there for the wawa next time I go to the dead zone. Next time I'm near a truck stop, I'll get that down like you have. You know that big truck platform so well from trucking horses and hay north with The Junior in the old days."

"Lots of Waffle Houses, Chrome, another good metaphor. I think using Waffle House for the vacuous state works well with

127

your 'wawa.' Like you said, schoolteacher, 'it's fungible.' I think from now on, I'll say I'm in the Waffle House when the blank lands come, waffling. I'll listen for the big trucks to back off, and I'll just waffle down to zero."

"Okay, you do that, Head Wound. What about your CB radio and the Ghost of Channel 19? Isn't that where you and The Junior first heard that term 'finished' you say at the end of your sentences?"

"Yeah, even you say 'finished' at the end of your sentences now, fucker. I've heard you. Goddamn, I miss The Junior. Feenished. That's the way he said finished, with that accent of his."

"I miss him, too. You doing to the sky what I am – open eye, closed eye, different sky?"

"Yes. Open eye, closed eye, different sky. That, and some good dream punk."

"Let's shut up for a while."

"Can you get to the boom box?"

"Probably. Might take an hour. Well, might seem like an hour. It's three feet away."

Chrome sat up and put on the Pearls Before Swine cassette, the band they listened to when they did this drug, the song that asked if they had, "Come by again to die again, well try again, another time," their cat-scan for cerebral screw worms. If you could get through that song and leave it, then you must be okay. The song meant a book title to Aubrey, whatever the book he wasn't writing was. He heard that line when things were so good, and yet he wondered what he was doing here, and when things were so bad he wanted to die, but "Try again another time."

DID YOU COME BY AGAIN

"You still do the projectamenta the way you used to?" Aubrey asked.

128

TO DIE AGAIN

"When you trombone Wonder Dog out to the end of the horn, then come back to a Waffle house to rest then back out again for another drifty?"

WELL TRY AGAIN

"Yeah."

ANOTHER TIME

"Do it all the time if I can get the time. Feenished."

"Remember the 'back peal'? Past tense. We'd say, 'I'm going to the back peal, the drive-by, again and again, over and over, changing what happened after something happened, going back and doing or saying something different the first time we were there."

TRY AGAIN, ANOTHER TIME

"You know it. Hey, can we turn the boom box down?"

"Sure. Hey, Chromie, I learned how to do something quite different, kind of a vaccination against the Mess Hall monsters. Well, I mean, I read it somewhere in a *True* magazine. I learned how to dumb myself down so my carburation of late isn't as scary as it used to be."

"Maybe it's this fast fly we're doing right now, but I didn't get what you meant. Dumb what?" Chrome up on one elbow now.

"I mean, John, all this complex rationalizing and identifying we do to stay sane. There's nothing better than the superficial parts of life after you have erased the overload of deeper meaning. I mean, the deeper meaning always comes back, but there's this shrink somewhere – England, I don't know – who told his patients to quit glorifying their hallucinations and fears by thinking they're artistic angels. He said you should turn yourself into Bubba when the Mess Hall comes. Open a can of Vienna sausage and say some

129

Baptist blessing over it, eat a dumb desert like Jell-O. Don't do that rationalizing therapy people tell you to do over and over; that doesn't work. I mean, it circles back around and ambushes you. Bites your brainwashed-effort ass. What you think, finished?"

"Never thought of it that way. Dumb it down."

"Yeah, the rationalizing cure is like making the sign of the cross too much when you're a Catholic until you finally cross yourself. Over rationalizing until it's irrational again, you know. Finished."

"Magazine… Magazine all over that!"

"Hey, what about Dr. Brown, Chrome?"

"Which one? The brown smack from Mexico up our nose we used to do, or the neurosurgeon in Miami?"

"Miami."

"He's well. Always asks how you're doing. He calls you Head Wound, too, after he put that plate in your head."

"And his TMS machine? Still experimenting with that?"

"Yep. Three weeks ago, I'm in Coconut Grove at his place. We did some acid and played around with the machine. Hey, guess who is working at Miami Jackson that Brown runs into now and then?"

"Leda," Aubrey nodded.

"Yep, the swan woman herself. Strangleda, your ex-beloved. Figured somehow you knew that."

"And what about your old sparring partner, Rose Mothershed?"

"Living happily with Jeff Bridges, the Star Man, at the bottom of some crater in Arizona waiting for the spaceship to pick them up. Or maybe they have been picked up and are living on a beach like this on Neptune, Jeff's home planet."

"Unbelievable, huh? Hard to believe movies are that dangerous."

"I do miss her. She was a dime-piece, a beautiful thin-lipped woman."

They were quiet for a while, until Aubrey said, "John."

"What?"

"You still like teaching school?"

"Yes. Love/hate sometimes. I mean, takes pounds of patience to keep loving them, especially the irremediable ones that make me want to turn into an amnesiac. I was thinking about my senior class on a coffee the other day, and it went a little negative, you know? Turned on me. Some days it's all coffee and love for them, but the other day I was thinking, I don't know, they seem to have these swollen cases of RIGHT NOW! and that gets to me. I watch them in the cafeteria. They eat too fast. I'm sitting there wondering fast, fast, fast lousy lovers, fast lousy eaters, fast drivers, fast lousy readers coming at you, America. All they seem to care about is what happens next. What used to be introspection in the old days is extrospection now. It's their fascination with these electronic adjuncts the gods of lucre sell them that do all that shit outside their minds – the computers, the phones, and other external wands. They live more outside their mind than inside it. Of course, maybe what we do isn't that healthy, either – you and me, living mostly inside it. And then I said to myself, 'You aging creep, this is what your old man thought you were like, and look how I turned out. I have a job I love, I get laid now and then, and I get to do this strong-ass dope on the beach and talk to the tower with my best friend. So I say to myself, shut up about the kids and keep filling their ears with the left pearls, and see how they do then, with their 'right now' shit!'"

They were quiet again.

"What's going on with Triple Suiter, that glorious piece of noumenon?" Chrome asked.

"Trip's here, sitting in the back of my head with his Underwood typewriter man, the Amper Sand. He leaves me alone when I do dope."

"You do so well with all that."

"Yeah, considering I think all our minds are populated with dead people called slippers."

"Well, they are. Virginia Woolf thought so, and Bellow did. And Nabokov was always talking about the 'democracy of the dead' in our head. There's something I never told you."

"What, English teacher? Me, your best friend?"

"Remember I told you I was a Catholic and went to Loyola, and I do all that Latin stuff with you when we're fucking around."

"What?"

"I went to Loyola, but I'm a Jew."

"Hope you're proud."

"Sure. I just know all that Catholic stuff because I went to college there like a lot of Jew-boys. Your Leda, the other Jew, the nurse at Miami Jackson, almost caught me one time when she said, *'Chabot Shalom'* on a Friday sunset at The Blue Goose. I was drunk and responded. I think she knew, really."

"Well, good. Now you and I can go at this messianic stuff we discuss from different angles, fixing religion and all the glorious substitutions for it we've acquired since we're too cool to believe it anymore. I mean, it seems like the Catholics educated me right out of their religion. Looks like we were hustled as little boys once by the god you were talking about earlier, who says he's the only one and ain't puttin up with no other Macaronis. *Mazel tov*, then, Chrome. You practiced in the art of deception, motherfucker. So after all these years you're? Well, rock our souls in the bosom of Abraham. Let's go back in the water and surf, Christ-killer. I'll baptize you."

"Too late. I let this wacked out *shikse* girl baptize me in college one night for a piece of ass. Finished."

They weren't finished. They had to stop at The Blue Goose for open mic night. Young guys got up and did rap – a new genre catching on – kind of a social comment crambo young people thought they invented, but the real seasoning in American culture, the season that has meant the most, the black additive, had been doing something called the "talking blues" for a century before the kids started rapping, and there were a lot of kids at the Goose tonight, white *and* black.

Chrome got Aubrey to get up and do one of his old rhymes because he could see he was uninhibited in his present chemical state from the beach. Aubrey used to play music there with his old band, Cricket Jar.

The place went quiet. They thought this old guy might sing some Neil Diamond. But of course, a lot of the older townies knew Aubrey Shallcross and wanted to know what was coming. In the old coffee house style of Ginsburg, Aubrey gave them lyrics from a talking blues song he had written two years ago. A song about how the whites tricked the blacks into killing each other by keeping them supplied with crack and guns. The poem was meant to send a message – not to be fooled by the white man.

"SOUTHSIDE CRIPS, NORTH SIDE BLOODS,

HATE EACH OTHER, DEATH IN THE HOOD.

BLUE'S ONE COLOR, RED'S ANOTHER.

YOU KILL A FRIEND; YOU KILL A BROTHER.

CRIPS HATE BLOODS; BLOODS HATE CRIPS

THE WHITE MAN'S LAUGHING, SELLS 'EM SHIT.

AND THE WHITE MAN, HE SAY,

PACK UP ALL MY CARES AND WHOA

HERE I GO, SINGING LOW

BYE, BYE, BLACKBIRD.

WHY, WHY, BLACKBIRD?

EVEN THE SKIN HEADS TOLD EACH OTHER

DON'T KILL A MAN WHEN HE'S YOUR COLOR.

SO, ASK YOUR MENTOR. ASK YOUR MOM.

FLIP IT OVER; IT'S UNCLE TOM.

FINISHED!"

The black kids in the place cocked their heads. Aubrey wasn't sure they got the message. It was a left pearl, the ones Chrome and he had talked about on the beach.

When he got home, Christaine had the smile. "Well, how was it? And how was John Chrome?"

"It was good, and Chrome was on top today. Some of that shit he says levels me. We stopped by the Goose and listened to the kids do rap. Chrome says the king's English has really slipped since the word 'fuck' replaced all the verbs and adjectives in the lexicon."

"Let me guess. Want a valium to come down?"

"Please, my love, and a double Bombay Sapphire and tonic."

"Fever Tree?"

"Yes, please, with you upstairs."

"Fever Tree?"

"I love you, Christaine. You're such of a woman, such of a woman. I often wonder how I ever talked you into sleeping with

134

an ugly like me. I used to plan out the sessions. I thought if she's going to let me, I'm going to have to be the world's most creative ugly lover."

"That's right. And it all started in the old house up the road. You with that confederate army uniform you'd put on and that sand hill crane outfit you used to flap around in naked, and then asking me to put on those angel wings you had in the closet. So get your nice tight casserole ass upstairs, and we'll find some outfits."

He lay there, after. Christaine was asleep. The night throb came with the film people. "Pick a film Aubrey, any film," they whined.

All these years, and Chrome told him today he was a Jew, not a Catholic. Aubrey told the voices, "Bring me *The Apprenticeship of Duddy Kravitz*. I wanna see Richard Dreyfuss."

"Yes, Aubrey," the voices said.

Down to The Trazadone Lounge he slid, where he stepped off a train in the Catskills for the summer with Duddy and was gone.

PART THREE

Chapter 20: ASSAULT ON SERMON

AM Sermon bought 1,500 hundred more acres that bordered Aubrey's place. It was the last stretch of pure pine palmetto and wetlands east of US 1, running all the way to the Atlantic Ridge, overlooking the town of Jensen Beach. Many species lived in those woods, delimited on all sides by other development and highways. Aubrey felt like a treasure was being squandered and decided to help the citizenry fight to make it a park.

He went to county commission meetings during the disputation and approval stages. It looked like the protests were delaying the project for at least another six months. At one meeting, he read a speech:

"There is noticeable concern over this project among longtime residents and newcomers. We care about what our county offers us and the environment. You call it North Jensen Beach, but it has nothing to do with Jensen Beach. Jensen Beach is a town. This is a wilderness, a beautiful one, and the Jensen beach part is out on Hutchinson Island, so the name is not even close to the feel of those acres. You are just doing this to get the word 'beach' on a billboard to attract sales. It reminds me of other developments I've seen in Florida. Deer Run, but there *are* no deer. Forest Hills, only there is *no* forest anymore, and there never were any hills. Or Holly Hill Heights, a project built on low land. No holly, either. Well, there's Florida holly – Brazilian peppers, of course." The crowd laughed.

"The area being considered tonight is populated with native fauna and flora, and this is the last piece like it east of US 1 in the county. These things we call the last of: the passenger pigeon, the ivory-billed woodpecker, *The Last Picture Show*. We saved

137

the Lyric Theatre downtown after its last movie, so why can't we do the same with the land? Don't forget the word 'sacred' and what it means to have those woods for our citizens and children to enjoy. Remember the old saying: 'The Lord helps those who help themselves.' Well, I don't think the Lord helps those who help themselves to everything. Thank you."

The audience applauded. The commissioners *for* the project were dour. The ones *against* the project smiled and nodded to each other. Someone sitting behind Aubrey leaned forward and asked if he'd run for county commissioner.

At home, Aubrey and Christaine talked until midnight about the developer's intentions and wondered what made him, AM Sermon, tick. In the corner of a bar in downtown, Sermon talked to his lawyer, a man who had gone to school with Aubrey and knew Aubrey's family, a man he hired to get his development through the approval stages because the lawyer was local.

"As council and a friend, of course, AM, I would advise you not to take Aubrey Shallcross and his connections too lightly. He is not the country boy he seems to be. Some people are actually a little scared of him. He's got a reputation for being strange and unpredictable."

But Sermon had his connections, too, connections capable of anything from graft to murder – the family in the Carolinas ruled by Big Jim Lovill, the silent partner on these projects, and Big Jim had someone in the Florida county to check on his money.

A week later, another hearing on the project was held, and attorneys for Sermon suggested Aubrey's land next to the development was not qualified for the agriculture zoning it enjoyed, ignoring the grandfather clause that gave it the original status. This made Aubrey mad and worried. He hired his own lawyer in case the developer asked for a hearing in front of a judge on the matter. Aubrey's lawyer found out during discovery that the other investor, Big Jim, had borrowed against large amounts of cash he kept in the vaults of a Canadian bank and was funneling it into the project to clean the money. The addresses on the account belonged to the Lovills in North Carolina, spread out among three tobacco auction warehouse companies in the counties surrounding Winston Salem.

The morning after the issue with his own land arose, Aubrey went to Asante's farm to school his dressage horse, Saxon.

"Good morning, Monsieur. Ready to assume the position? Ready to supple your horse for the next Olympics?"

"In my dreams."

"You never know, Aubrey. You're starting to learn this dressage pretty well, even for a cowboy. My daughter tells me the county is after you."

"Yes. And some of my business friends from the old days say I'm a turncoat, siding with the tree huggers and horizonites."

"And you? Do you think you are?"

"Enough is enough of this building craze. I did well in the car business because of all the growth here, but I sold out because I thought this place was built out. I'm against further density. You can't even get around town anymore."

"It's okay, Aubrey. Maybe you can go into politics if you don't go to the Olympics for dressage," Asante laughed.

It was time to go camping. He rode the ranch mare to the spot on the creek, set up like he did before, and sat down to talk to his mental companion. "This fire is stupid enough, Trip. It's about seventy-eight degrees tonight. Looks good, though, don't it? Doo lang, doo lang."

"Yes, decorous. A nice prop. Sets are important. Shall we sing some more James Taylor?"

"I don't know. We came out here because you want to help me with something that has to do with the creatures I see around this fire pit. I told no one about this, for fear of being committed, right?"

Trip said nothing. He didn't have to. Aubrey knew the answer. When it was time, he swallowed his two fifty-milligram Trazadones and went down to the lounge to come up with a movie. He woke at five in the morning, when the two gators, the armadillo, the coach whip, and their slippers came to the campsite. Trip was standing with them at the end of Aubrey's arm, and all the slippers were smiling and nodding, even the sometimes-sullen Osceola. Nemo walked out of his gator's eye onto its nose to address the group.

"This is the time, my friends. The county commission will vote on the Jensen Beach project. We have come to ask, Mr. Shallcross, if you will speak the night before the vote is taken. If they vote to approve, we will start the war. If they are swayed by the protests and your speech, then we will rest with a vigilant eye."

"I can't give you much hope they will listen, Captain Nemo," Aubrey said, "given the record over the last twenty years of project approvals in this county."

"Please try. You are our only human way to their conscience, and even if they don't listen and vote *for* it, what you have to say before the vote will become a matter of record, and we hope will touch the collective conscience of the people when the next project is proposed."

"I'll try. I will try. Could I ask one more thing, Captain Nemo? And this involves Martha here with us tonight."

"Certainly."

"It seems Martha and I have friends in common. Roberta and Speedy from the carnival."

"My Roberta?" Martha said.

"Yes. The same. I want to bring them into this like you brought me and Freddie Tommie into it. I think they are trustworthy and would be valuable assets."

Martha went over and spoke to Nemo. Nemo thought for a moment and then agreed, as long as Martha vouched for them. The next night, Aubrey spoke to the commissioners.

"Commissioners, Mr. Sermon, my fellow citizens. There is a dangerous view of some, in this county's wherewithal. Some think that anything that creates jobs and makes money is approvable. I acknowledge these things are essential if done responsibly, but I am reminded of the old saying, 'a dog in the manger,' a metaphor for useless excess, for overeating something you don't even like. Dogs don't belong in mangers. They don't eat oats. Mangers belong to cattle and horses, but some dogs won't let it go. No, they just sit in the manger on top of the oats and corner what is not necessary to them, what is inedible to them, just to lord over it for the power and possession. This project is a manger meant for people, for a park, not the dogs that want power and money. The developers are not even going to live there in the end. It is the last piece of untouched wild between US 1 and the watershed at the base of the Atlantic Ridge. I am asking, for the people's sake, the commission vote no tonight and save this area for the county and those who will visit here in the future. There is land more suitable than this for homes. This land is one of a natural kind, gone forever if you approve it."

The vote was postponed for a week. Whether they wanted to think about what the speakers had to say that night or were just faking a stall to make the public think they were being careful, no one knew. In the end, they approved it. The county wanted the increased tax base to pay for already-behind infrastructure other projects were supposed to complete before this one got approved and as usual, they hadn't. This was supposed to be against the law, but they found ways around it. Much to the delight of the local building trades, preliminary work began. The country boys changed oil in their front-end loaders and bulldozers. They felled trees and pushed away the rich topsoil at the direction of the various job superintendents.

Out on the other project, Cypress Prairie, two large ponds had been dug as deep as they could be, for valuable fill to build roads and raise lots. It was illegal to penetrate the marl layer close to the precious aquifer below and contaminate the ground water. Here, Nemo and Osceola would start their campaign of extreme action, the kind of surreal action Greenpeace wished they had available, the most unimaginable of eco-warriors – alligators, snakes, animals, and animatronic partnerships, captained by the ghosts of famous people.

In the dark of darks, under a clouded sky lit only by the bounce-back of downtown streetlights two miles away, the big gators moved on the creek to Cypress Prairie to continue their work. A tall, tough Indian stood on their backs; something only another Indian or white witchcraft could explain to a white.

"What did I tell you?" history murmured from under the water to Freddie Tommie, who was wearing the big gator skull over his head, dressed above the waist in war paint, the tooth-studded cane knives in his hands, the knives with turquoise inlays shinning like blue dimes of hell.

Behind him stood the armadillo on The Dragon. The eight-foot snake lay coiled on the back of Two-Toed Tom while the Gypsy lady, Martha, sat inside the snake's yellow eyes, singing something in Roma. It was a vision from the top of Aubrey's blindspot cathedral – peyote in the paint, calling out for justice from the Breath Master and Wakon Tonka.

"See, what'd I tell ya?" the earth whispered to the old Indian mounds.

"What'd I tell ya?" it said to the bones of Ponce De Leon.

"What'd I tell ya?" it said to the old crackers buried on stolen land.

"What'd I tell ya?" it said as it knocked on Henry Flagler's grave and the southern angels sang, "We told you so," down to the Army Core of Engineers.

Like the chariot Caesar, Freddie came down the waterway standing on fifteen hundred pounds of live U-boat, to attack Sermon and anyone else who made lesions of the land.

Chapter 21: THE RELIABLY UNRELIABLE
NARRATOR, TRIPLE SUITER

I've been thinking about Sermon – me, the tracer, the go-between, Triple Suiter. How I know him, how maybe he's not all villain, just another terrified narcissist like Aubrey's friend Arquette, from the other book, the *Flame Vine* story.

It is the southern winter, carnival show season. One night, AM does the carnival late. Vito is about to put Kong, his big male chimp, out to fight. Vito named him Kong, of course, for show appeal. The ape reminds AM of the way people see *him* and the way he sees himself – admired and despised. He grew up in the city of Greensboro, North Carolina. His mother's maiden name was Murrow, and she told him they were related to the famous TV and radio newsman Edward R. Murrow. Also from the town: O'Henry, Charles Kuralt, Soupy Sales, and Charlie Rose. "There's something in the water in Greensboro," she told him.

AM was sent to Guilford, the local college founded by the Quakers. The football team was called the Fighting Quakers, an inside oxymoron joke. AM was on the football team, the boxing team, the baseball team, and the debate team; he got a degree in business administration. His ethics teacher was a strong influence on the way he justified behavior. What was the greater good? When he was up for the Vietnam draft, he showed the draft board pictures of himself as a boxer covered in blood; in his football uniform, dirt-caked with more blood, then a picture of his tiny, thin mother in front of the little grocery store she ran on her own after his father's death when he was nineteen. "I'm an only child," AM said to the draft board. "My mother struggled without me in the store alone so I could finish college, and I will not leave her to kill herself working while I'm in the service. You can see from my history in sports that I am not afraid to fight, but I consider my responsibility to my mother's life and our only source of income the higher ground." The board bought it and let him out. Gave him a hardship pass to stay out of the war. It was his first taste of outthinking the law outside of Guilford College.

It was a cool Florida night at the carnival. The ape came to the corner with his two handlers, ready to fight. Vito went to the center of the ring without a microphone and started daring the audience to send someone up. Vito was slightly drunk. He slipped once, trying to get around in the fighting cage.

The first man to fight was Vito's shill, and they put on another apocryphal show to make the audience believe the man almost won. When the match was over, Kong looked out at the audience and then directly at AM in the front row. A man from the audience flicked a cigarette at the ape. AM turned and looked hard at the man. Another man reached through the bars and pulled the hair on the ape's leg, and when he tried it again, AM grabbed his hand and bent it backward until the man went to his knees and cowered away. Kong stared more at AM. AM thought he saw the simian smile, but he was not sure. He only knew that was the beginning of his platonic relationship with the ape, and he went every other night to watch him fight and was the only one to cheer for Kong instead of the sucker who gave Vito the hundred to go in there.

Out of college, AM was hired by a huge Miller beer distributor. The owner of the company promoted him when he suggested the company use the slogan "Champagne of Bottled Beer," because the growing Hispanic population in the south could say the word *champagnia* in Spanish very easily, but it was a jaw breaker for them to pronounce the competitor's name, Budweiser. Later, the whole Miller Brewing Company adopted the slogan.

From there, AM went out on his own. With his acquisitive drive, he built an empire of slogans used in the vitamin and supplement trade charade, then added the "as seen on TV" business for other telegenic products. He told someone, "I learned all my negotiating skills arguing with my insufferable wife." But he was in a bit of trouble now and could not appreciate the ambit of it. The government was charging him with mail fraud. He claimed his flagship product, jojoba oil, from a plant in the Southwest, would grow hair, and that it was the reason Indians in Arizona had all their hair. When he shipped the product through the US Post Office, it became federal and got their attention.

He continued to be fascinated with Kong. He'd loved boxing as a young man and he kept that famous cartoon of an ape holding a human skull, pondering its evolution instead of the other way around, on his desk at the office.

As the carnival fight spectacle was in its second match that night, the animal army of Captain Nemo was three miles away, just outside the gates of Cypress Prairie, an army captained by the spirits of our own kind, slippers, after they passed through the universe to a windmill with a larger breeze.

Freddie stepped off the backs of the alligators onto the bank and followed the monsters through the woods to a corner on the south side of the project. They waited. Martha, the Gypsy, rode her armadillo to a corner on the north side; her eight-foot coach whip followed. The armadillo sat on his hind legs and snapped his toenails together; a spark flew and lit the pine needles and grass on fire. Martha left the armadillo through its nose, and went through the nose of her coach whip beside the armadillo. Once seated in its eyes, the snake flew down the road to the construction trailer where the night guard sat outside eating a sandwich. The plan was to get the guard to turn his attention, so The Dragon and Tom could enter the ponds and work their own plan on the thin bottoms.

Martha had her snake grab its tail in its mouth and make a myth come true: It stood up in the shape of a hoop and rolled past the guard like a child pushing a wheel rim with a stick. The guard's mouth dropped. He followed the snake with his eyes as it circled and went by again. The fire Martha started with her armadillo began to burn higher. The guard saw it and jumped in his golf cart to go investigate, still looking back at the rolling snake.

The big gators entered the pond. They dove towards the deepest part jamming their noses into the bottom where the marl was. There they spun their muscular tails above them and became living drills, while A.M. watched his ape spin at the show grounds, then knock a man down.

It only took a minute for the gators to break through to the aquifer below, collateral damage necessary to stop the project. The proctors of such things, the inspectors and the building department, would close it down when they discovered the aquifer was breeched. Kong hit his opponent again, hard. AM was on his feet while the rest of the crowd cheered for the man to get up, but he was done. The handlers pulled Kong back with the ropes attached to the head gear. A single bloody human tooth was on the canvas.

The gators moved to the next pond and did the same to the bottom. The security guard only saw the fire and was beside himself on the phone to the fire department. The animal army gathered again on the south side of the property and returned to the creek, where Freddie stood waiting. The land creatures climbed on board the gators, and they all left on the water.

AM went home that night in a good mood, his man Kong – and that's the way he thought of him, a *man* like him – beat every opponent, and even came to the corner and stared at AM again. AM kept his phone number unlisted, so it was not until the next day, inspectors told him of the breeches in the aquifer and the mysterious fire that started on a corner of the property. The county shut the project down until the expensive process of draining the ponds and repairing the holes could be completed. AM blamed the site work contractor for digging the ponds too deep, and the contractor blamed his men. The other theory was the Zarnitz boys from the neighboring ranch had sneaked in, lit the fire, and then breeched the pond bottoms.

"But how could they drill through without a piece of obvious huge equipment?" AM asked his wife on the phone that night.

In the week that followed, AM was subpoenaed by the grand jury in Palm Beach County to answer questions. They wanted proof his mail order baldness treatment had efficacy. Was he duping the public and using the United States mail as a conduit?

The atmosphere at Cypress Prairie was awful for a while. The job superintendent saw the gator tracks going in and out of the ponds, but he didn't think it meant anything. This was Florida. He didn't notice one track showed only two toes on a front foot.

The day came, not only for AM to answer to the grand jury, but for Vito to answer to the Humane Society. In the crowd the other night, as AM swooned over the marvels of his agile ape while his construction project was attacked, an undercover man watched the carnival fight play out. The sheriff couldn't protect Vito anymore, and there was an investigation after a judge allowed a search warrant.

Vito called the show people together and said he wanted to move the winter quarters to another town. He wanted to run. He said he had discussed it with the show's majority owner in Ohio, who agreed to it. The show people thought this was crazy and would be personally costly to them, and they had their own meeting without Vito. Speedy talked to the majority owner in Ohio, and it turned out that the owner had not approved relocating the show. In fact, he would love for someone to rid him of Vito, he said, as the King of England once said he would love someone to rid him of his archbishop.

Vito and Roberta knew lots about Vito's sexual activity and substance affinity, because The Girl with No Joints had entertained them with stories; she was a favorite pastime of Vito's, and he paid her well for performances in his trailer. It became a crisis to save the show itself, and was viewed by Roberta and Speedy the way AM viewed everything – what was the greater good?

The Girl with No Joints came to Speedy and Roberta two days later. Vito had beaten her in a drunken fit for no reason. "No one does that to me," she said, and told them she had an idea how to send Vito away. Vito's "thing" was getting high on bath salts while he sat drunk in a warm tub; he liked her to put her ankles behind her head to let him play man with his hand. She didn't say anymore, and neither did Speedy and Roberta. Two days later, with the ape show closed, The Girl with No Joints bought bath salts and started to rub up to Vito again. He half apologized for beating her while the tub in his trailer was filling.

While he cooked in the tub, the girl let him parry his wrist and handled his Abraham. Because she knew what she was going to do, it was easier to deal with the disgust. His eyes closed, head back, mouth open, the no joints girl reached for the box of bath salts and quietly dumped the whole thing in the water. Her job was to wake him when he passed out and get him to bed. Not tonight. Bath salts can kill you. Not tonight. The next day, 911 took his body past Kong's cage while The Girl with No Joints sang some childish song and practiced her tumbling in the morning air between sips of a confection coffee.

ANIMAL SLIPPERS

Chapter 22: THE SWALLOW

The boy had gone into his parents' room. Aubrey's toadstone ring was on the nightstand. He sat on the side of the bed, put the ring on a finger, and moved his hand back and forth and made airplane sounds like he and his father made on the shell rock road. His father told him the ring had special power. "Mansion power." Drayton didn't know why, but he thought to put the ring in his mouth and just hold it there after he had seen and touched it, to give the taste sensation a shot at knowing it. He didn't mean to; it just slipped back in his throat and he reflex- swallowed it past his windpipe, where it lodged above his stomach before the pyloric valve and began to spasm.

Christaine, so scared, picked him up and put him in the car. A dark line shelf cloud was coming from the south towards town.

With Drayton screaming every time a spasm came, and Christaine driving as fast as was safe, they hit the first line of rain and boom! She didn't remember.

"I never heard of lightning harming anyone in a car," Aubrey said to the deputy at the hospital.

"We think what happened here, Mr. Shallcross, was it fried the electrical system. It didn't really harm her, but it killed the engine, the power steering, and the power brakes. She lost control and crashed into some trees."

The doctor came. "She's hit her head. We are doing a CAT scan to see if there is a bleed. She's in and out of consciousness.

Your son is fine. There was a gastroenterologist in the ER when the ambulance brought them. At first, we couldn't figure out what was wrong because every time he tried to tell us, another spasm stopped him from talking. We got an x-ray, and there was that ring, stuck above the stomach. Dr. Miller gave him a strong sedative and was able to reach it with the scope. Drayton is still in the recovery room. They'll come get you as soon as he is awake. Here's the ring. Odd ring. I've never seen one quite like it."

"Can I see *her*?"

"They have her upstairs in radiology. It could be a little while before she's back in ICU. I'll have a nurse come and get you."

He was shaking. He sat in the waiting room. "Trip, I'm not all right. My son – his throat – they reached down his throat like they did mine when I was his age after I swallowed those things, and I've been crooked by it ever since. He swallowed my ring, Trip!"

"He will be fine, Aubrey. They removed it."

"No, don't you see it? He swallowed it because he wanted to, because he had to. He's like me. He's got it, Trip, the pica, the stupid compulsion. He wanted to swallow it 'cause he couldn't stop himself."

"Let's wait and see what the details are."

An older woman sitting in the waiting room looked at him. "You all right, son? You have a loved one that's sick?"

"Accident. My wife, sort of. Not really married. Just very much in love," he said, his voice breaking.

"I'm thinking that's better than most married, now days. She gonna be all right?"

"They seem to think so. They always start out telling you that."

"What kind of accident was it?"

"Lightning hit the car. She was taking my son to the emergency room and lightning hit the car."

"Is your boy all right?"

"Long story."

"You're Aubrey Shallcross, aren't you?"

"Yes, ma'am," he said, his voice still breaking.

"I remember you used to own Shallcross Chrysler."

"Yes, ma'am."

"Well, all we can do is sit with it. Like most things in life we can't do nothin about, learnin to sit with things is somethin you got to figure out."

Aubrey remembered the river man Coker Barnes saying the same exact thing once. He dug his fingers into the arm of the chair. His mind saw row after row of roadkill crosses along a highway. Even Triple Suiter was quiet, as if a distraction of this size could distract the most perfected of beings and move everything in Aubrey's split mind into just one Camelot, one hemisphere. Only the perfected schizophrenic could manage the move to the singular seat like that, something he did in a crisis his whole life when he needed to without medicine. Then the discipline failed and spread out bicameral in his brain again.

"Trip, I'm gonna freak. I know it. It's coming. *He* is coming. It's because I shot those blue jays out of the tree when I was a kid, a whole family of them, and now my family is being punished for it. He's coming, Trip. I can feel it."

"No, stop it with that old blue jay guilt you always dredge. I can't believe you brought that up; it's so stupid it still bothers you. Listen to me, Aubrey. You know what to say to yourself. It's self-talk here, what you and I do when this happens. Repeat with me, *toro feces* and *veritas*, *toro feces* and *veritas*, bullshit and truth, just like our fix in the old days. Say it! Chicken shit, chicken salad."

Aubrey began to mouth the words.

"Good, that's it." Trip was out on Aubrey's arm now, leading the lines. "*Toro feces* and *veritas*, bullshit and truth, righty tighty lefty loose. You know it, Aubrey, the great quid, the way of the world. There's only *True* magazine and the rest is for tickets, trollers, and spinners trying to sell you bullshit."

"Trip, my family, they need me. Don't let me crater. The Slim Hand, he was coming. I could hear him counting just now. 'One Mississippi.' I thought he was coming, and I was going back to the top of the old church so he could stick his hand down my throat like that doctor did to my son an hour ago."

"No, Aubrey. No black church, no Blind Spot Cathedral today. Hear me? We're not going to let him come. You are okay. Try not to breathe for a second. Let your body get rid of some oxygen."

"My boy's in here tonight, too," the lady in the waiting room said, looking for something in her purse, instead of at Aubrey. "He got hit by lightning last year like your sorta-wife, but he got his nose broke today by this mean kid in town. I mean, I call him my boy. He's thirty-five years old. He's a special needs person, and that nose a-his is bad broke. They's having to operate to put it back right."

Aubrey just sat on the bottom of somewhere. Managed a nod. The lady picked up the coffee next to her, then pulled out a tin of Copenhagen and put a pinch in her lip. "Yeah, that boy a-mine, oh Lord, is like an egg got broke in his head when he's born. I could see it when he's a baby. Wouldn't look nobody in the eye, even when he's a-layin on his back. Just keep staring at the ceiling and when he *would* look at you, is like a cat what looks at you, but ain't lookin at you. Know what I mean? We named him Dewitt after his daddy, rest his soul, and we call him Dewey for short, like we did his daddy, us havin' the last name of Drinkard. We thought it cute, you know? Dewey Drinkard. Now later on, we called him Half Track, cause he loves his brother Darnell's halftrack swamp buggy so much. That was after the doctors told us Dewey was gone-minded and was a autism." She stopped, squeezed her lips, and spit her snuff in a drink can. "And I'm his mother, so I'm gonna love him, and God loves him, even though Dewey used to not want nobody to kiss or hug him, cause he's a autism type, you know. And now that he got sparked in that storm by lightning last year and woke up two days later, he started looking at people when they talk. Even lets you hug him a little. I don't know! Mighta fixed that broke egg. Yeah, two weeks ago, they give him a job sweepin over at the tow truck place. Course, it was the county what got him the work. One a-them people what looks out for people like him that ain't right, you know. His first real job, oh Jesus, and he's thirty-five years old. I went out to the cemetery and told his daddy. There's a nice little picture of his daddy on the headstone, him in his thirties in a white suit and wide tie. Damn cancer."

"Sparked? You mean lightning?" Aubrey asked, straightening out some.

"Yeah. 'Member? I told you a minute ago. Just like your wife, I mean sorta your wife. Maybe it'll make her one a-them people what can see things we can't after this. You know, see what things really look like, 'stead a-what we think they look like."

"Guess I was, or I didn't hear you. Did it hit him directly, the lightning?"

"Well, it hit a tree next to the half-track when they was out huntin, and it jumped to him when he was a-holdin onto that metal tower."

"When was that again?"

"Last year. It changed him, swear. That's how come they give him a job at the tow truck place – cause he started acting half human, but only half. Mighta reset his head a bit, the doctor said.

Maybe your sorta-wife be able to figure mysteries after this," she said, and she smiled, trying to make Aubrey smile.

"You know my name. Now what's yours?"

"I'm Betty Drinkard. My son, Darnell, is foreman of the Harris Ranch."

"Yes. I've never met your son, but I do know the ranch from when I was a kid, and I've heard his name at the cattle sale in Okeechobee."

"Well, we are all real happy about Dewey gettin better and gettin that job at the tow-truck place. He works with a man named Bob. Bob drives tow trucks to the wrecks, and Dewey rides with him to help hook up. When they go to a wreck and there's a fatality, Bob puts up one a-them roadkill crosses he keeps in the tow-truck for the family with his card on it, you know, so the family can call him and order a nicer cross what he makes in the shop out back a-his house."

Aubrey blacked out.

Trip could do nothing after the old lady said, "Roadkill cross." The Slim Hand came counting, "One Mississippi, two Mississippi…" Aubrey went through the flank muscle curtains to the Blind Spot Cathedral. Red men stabbed hooks on wires through his hands and hoisted him, arms out like his old Jesus in the deltoid hell of the gymnast cross. Up and up they took him to the top of the black church like a *Man Called Horse*, where the scar, the great cicatrix, used to be turning like a whirlpool, but the hole was open now from the bullet he took two years ago. Aubrey flew through the hole out to the universe beyond the sun. He went through so fast, streaking to the Milky Way, the Slim Hand had no time to cram the large object down his throat. He stopped at the in-vitro baby orbiting the old spaceship Stanley Kubrick and *2001* put there. He curled in a ball, put his thumb in his mouth, twirled his hair, and joined the space baby once known as Bowman.

They called a code in the hospital. Picked him up off the floor of the waiting room, put him on a gurney, and jumped on his body with electrodes, thinking he'd had a heart attack. Lines on a screen read out a stray, unusual calm. One medico said he had never seen this before after what must have been a seizure, this normal heartbeat. Aubrey and Trip continued to recite their old rhyme and circle the old spaceship and the space baby.

"WHEN YOU CAN'T SEE, TAKE A STRAIGHT SHOT,

RIGHT THROUGH THE HEART OF THE BLIND SPOT.

TRUE MAGAZINE KNOWS THE TRUTH,

RIGHTY TIGHTY, LEFTY LOOSE!"

Aubrey came to. The hospital people tried to tend to him. The calm left him, and he started to scream, then passed out again and went back two years ago, dying in a truck's back seat, blood running from his head after Carlos shot him. Christaine's family raced him to the hospital on US 1. He managed to look through the windshield and saw them – roadkill crosses by the hundreds – lined up in rows like Georgia pine trees. Then the crosses disappeared under the front bumper of the truck, and he did, too, into his coma.

Tonight, Betty Drinkard, still spitting into her drink can, watched as a doctor injected Aubrey with Thorazine, the same drug the Blue Goose bunch took to the beach in the old days when they did acid in case someone freaked, and Leda, his young wife, freaked. She told Aubrey to make the acid stop. He promised it would soon, but it wasn't soon enough, and he had to stick her with the Thorazine. Now here he was, floating in another Waffle

House from the same drug, Christaine upstairs in the ICU with a head wound like him, and his son recovering from a pica episode after swallowing a large object. He tried to get upset, but the Thorazine wouldn't have it, as the sound of an eighteen-wheel semi coasting down for an exit inside his head let its Jake brake go, budadaddda.

"Waffle, waffle," he mumbled, moving his head from side to side.

A nurse asked what was waffle. John Chrome got there. Chrome said, "He says 'waffle,' to calm himself down. Or sometimes 'Wa, wa, wa,' you know, the sound a cavitating outboard motor makes in the wakes of other boats when it rocks." The nurse backed quickly away from Chrome.

"Aubrey. Aubrey, man. What the hell?"

"Christaine, John. Lightning. Ambrose Bierce, John, a head wound like Ambrose got in the war. A head wound like mine, John; she got a head wound, and Drayton, he swallowed it. The ring, my toadstone ring on the dresser in the house. I put that on him, John, that swallow thing. It came through the blood on him from me. Marked him up, god damn it, because of me," Aubrey chattered.

"Okay, you go back down, man. Close your eyes, will you? Listen for the sounds. Hear them? Wa, wa, wa, wa."

"Thorazine they gave me, John."

"Listen for the Jake brake then, Aubrey. That'll calm you. You're outside a truck stop, budadaddda. The big trucks are slowing down for the exit. C'mon, man. C'mon!"

"If you don't quiet down, sir, I'm going to get security," a nurse said to Chrome.

"Calm down? I'm trying to calm this man down."

"I will call security."

Aubrey grabbed Chrome's hand. "John, do what she says. You try to stay here."

The other doctor came. "Your boy is awake in the recovery room. Your wife has a bleed, a brain hemorrhage. We don't know the extent of it, and we want to get her down to St. Mary's in West Palm. Mr. Shallcross, has she complained of headaches before this?"

"No. No."

"When we did the scan, we found another area in her brain that was not normal."

"God."

"Could be something congenital. Can't tell. Right now, the most important thing is to tend to the pressure created by the bleed."

"Can I see her?"

"Not in your condition. She is in an induced coma. Stay here until the Thorazine wears off. I'm surprised you can even talk after that shot. I will arrange for your wife to be airlifted to St. Mary's."

"Please, I'd like her sent to Miami Jackson. My own doctor, Henry Brown, is there. He's a neurosurgeon."

"We can do that. I've heard of him."

Chapter 23: LEDA AND ARQUETTE

In Miami, Aubrey's old childhood friend, Arquette, has come from Boston to see Leda. It's been ten years.

In Coconut Grove, they get coffee. Face to face, the few phone calls, all they know about the recent each other.

"Have you reenlisted in the Yankee army for good? Why did you leave Jensen Beach?"

"I ran. New England's home, you know. Where I'm from originally. It seemed the only chicken shit thing to do. Run."

"Pretty honest."

"And you?"

"Rehab like I said on the phone, I needed to clean. Somehow in Jensen Beach every time I got straight, I found myself looking up the ass of a narcotic again. I finally got turned around. I'm in my old nursing job at Jackson Surgical. Still live alone. Go out some and have a few girlfriends. Drink a little, but stay away from the white. Keep it simple, though I've had my slip-ups, like when I heard Aubrey was shot, I took a shot myself. Couldn't bring myself to call him, but still, it's easier to stay away from the Jane down here than it was up in Jensen. I was so into Aubrey, but I wouldn't tell him. I competed with him. Made me crazy, I guess."

163

"I was told by a girl that works summers where I live, he was shot in the head. She said he was lucky and seems fairly normal."

"Aubrey normal. That's royal. He has someone, and I understand he's happy. I'm happy for him. I heard they have a kid, too, so I thought I better stay down. Did you know it was her ex that shot him?"

"Yes. I heard he was a former cop and drug dealer from here."

"They brought Aubrey to Miami Jackson for surgery, but I wasn't there then."

"I'm embarrassed I didn't contact him, too, Leda."

"I know. I know. I don't live far from here. Wanna go?"

In the dark, Arquette said out of nowhere, "It took me a long time to realize it was a singular thing."

"What?"

"It was just me, my nuts, my body, the pathologic gym thing, the constant inventory, the sex I was obsessed with back then. I thought every royal palm tree looked like a French tickler, every sea grape leaf look like a gland, every round concrete bumper in a driveway with a piece of rebar through the middle looked like a breast and a nipple. And there was my body image problem. I've thought I looked physically undernourished since I was twelve years old. My parents had to intervene when I was in high school. I was sent to a therapist. Didn't work very well."

"Still like that? You're very fit and handsome, you know."

"Yeah, I'm still like that, but a lot less since I hit the wall in Jensen. I take a silver bullet now, an antidepressant."

"Which?"

"Celexa."

"Hey, me, too. You know there's no brand new anymore, Arquette. We're all used stuff. I'm tired."

She went to her room and him to his. They had never slept

together, only that weird voyeurism they used to practice – that naked touching themselves while they watched each other until they were done. Carlos, Aubrey's shooter, had palindromed once, "No son! Onanism's a gross orgasm sin – a no-no, son." Sin or not, that kind of masturbation apart, while they watched each other is what they did secretly while she was married to Aubrey. It was her idea, under the guise of physical therapy for Arquette's mysterious pelvic pain. She ran the sessions the way she tried to run everything. He had developed a fear of sex, sex where you touched someone, and sex and the gym were the only lids he had for his constant anxiety.

Sunday morning.

"Want breakfast, Arquette?"

They went to Wolfie's, the iconic local Jewish restaurant.

"Want me to order for you?"

"No. I know Jewish food. I went to Brown. Half the school is Hebrew, like you. The others are Asian, and me, the lone *goyim*."

"Right."

"Speaking of Jews, I've been reading a lot of Philip Roth lately. Roth said this thing I liked. It's well known. 'When some men make love to a woman, they get revenge for every failure in their life.'"

"Was that you?"

"Probably. It almost buried me, the rabid sex. It took years before I could start to look at women from the waist up and then the chin up. And now I have to look at my failures, too, from the chin up, or *with* my chin up."

They ate. She put down her fork. "What really made you decide to come down?"

"I miss. I miss all of it from back then, except the bad parts."

"You don't talk as much as you used to, Arquette."

"You don't, either."

"Okay, I'll pick it up on this coffee. The strangest thing happened this year. I was at work. A patient was on the table. He had a tattoo on his forearm, and it said, 'MIDGE.' I had seen this word before on a man's arm, a man we all knew back in Jensen Beach. In fact, *you* knew him; Aubrey told me you guys had known him since you were young. He had a bookstore in Stuart. His name was Sonny."

Arquette nodded, said he was a quiet loner, said Aubrey knew him better because at one time, Sonny had lived next door to him. "So, I'm listening."

"Well, I went to this patient's room the next day and asked him about the tattoo. He told me he had a habit of huffing Freon when he was younger. He said some huffers tattooed that word on their arms in honor of the man who discovered Freon – Thomas Midgley. They seemed to spell it differently. I checked it out."

"Uh?"

"Arquette, remember the Tin Snip Killer in Martin County and those women they found in old refrigerators? Remember? Ship in a Bottle was written in their blood on the doors."

"Of course. That started when I was really young. A girl in our class, Nell Kitching, her mother was cut up by that deviant. Nell lost her mind over that."

"Arquette, see where I'm going with this? They never found out who the killer was. What if it was Sonny? Those murdered women's lungs were full of Freon, I remember according to the autopsies. Sonny had MIDGE tattooed on his arm. I saw it in the bookstore one day when I was with Aubrey. What became of the guy? Is he still around?"

"Don't know. I left, remember? Could ask Aubrey."

"We'd have a lot to fix with him before we do that."

"Aw, c'mon. Let's call him while we're high on this coffee."

No one answered.

The next day, Leda went to the hospital cafeteria and ran straight into Aubrey. Leda, the old bandicooter. The potato thief. She sneaks into your garden, digs up your potatoes, then replants the nice green plant on top of the empty place where the potatoes were, like nothing happened – the great metaphor for adultery. That's the way the Irish tell it, and that's the way Leda was with her lovers, then she'd look Aubrey in the eye like a replanted potato plant, as if her fidelity and the potatoes were still there.

"What in hell!" she said to him sitting at a table.

"I'm here with Christaine," he said, staring at the floor.

"You have a little boy, too, I heard."

"You heard?"

"I know. I know. I'm terrible."

"Well, we stayed in touch at first, and then you quit."

"I, I just thought it better to butt out. Is she sick?"

"Accident with the car. The thing – I mean the car – got hit by lightning. She has a head injury. Anyway, they want to relieve the pressure, and I asked to bring her here so Henry Brown could do it."

"That's smart."

"Yeah, well, he took care of me when I came here."

"I know. I wasn't working here then. It was a head wound? A gunshot?"

"Yeah. They said I'm okay now."

Leda looked at him, and then they both were laughing. "You've never been okay, Aubrey, even before the gunshot. You've always had a head wound."

"Yeah, well, same to you, white girl."

"You in a band?"

"Lord, no. Getting too old to sing. I think about it a lot, but I just stopped. Hey, guess who's living in the guest house on the old place."

She shook her head.

"Nell Kitching. The girl in the institution, the one I grew up with and used to go see."

"And she is able to do it on her own?"

"Good as you and me, some kind of barely okay, I guess. Guess it's enough to get out of the crazy house. I mean we're all out, aren't we?"

They laughed again.

"Well, then your turn to guess. Who do you think just flew into Miami yesterday after all these years?"

Aubrey shook his head.

"The Viceroy of Venery, the Abbott of Ass, as John Chrome used to call him."

"Arquette. My goodness, what goes around *does* come around. That motherfucker hasn't called me in years, either."

"Honest, I haven't heard from him until now but a couple of times."

"Look, I gotta go see what's going on with Christaine."

"Of course. I love that name."

"You being a facetious Jew now?"

"Fuck you, Aubrey."

"Yeah. Sorry."

"I come to the cafeteria on my break every day at eleven for coffee."

Aubrey nodded and shrugged. She walked away.

"Trip. You heard all that?"

"I heard."

"Same Leda. Hadn't seen me in years. Kinda flippant about it."

"Not as flippant as you think. It's an act. She's an act; doesn't take anything that lightly, otherwise, she wouldn't be an addict."

Chapter 24: THE CHRISTAINE BRAIN

She was a spectacular rolled in gold, an angel not flying too close to the ground. When they first met at her parent's party, she had knelt on the floor with him and together they sang "The Battle Hymn of the Republic." They pretended to be shot Confederate soldiers and went down on their backs so they could die like nerve-gassed sheep on a military test range. The other guests at the party stared.

Five minutes later, they were out on the screened porch. She told him about turning the mannequin she found in a shed into an altar boy she had a crush on when she was thirteen, and secretly humping it in her tree house, though nothing happened from the sensation until she took it to a shell pit pool and came with it in the water. Her guilt from that was so Catholic, she ran crying with closed eyes into the side of a banyan tree. It split her lip in three places, and god, did Aubrey love the scars on those lips she wore. Now she was in a coma, like he had been two years ago.

Right before the accident, when lightning hit the car, she was writing a story about justifiable homicide and her view of modern-day mating; relationships in our culture versus relationships in wild history. It was a story of what a mother would do to protect her young.

She found herself in one of many tell-all conversations with Nell Kitching one day. She told Nell she would kill him again – Carlos, her ex-husband – pull that hat pin from her belt as he lay naked on top of her, trying to force his dysfunctional erection inside her, while her son was locked crying in a closet. Carlos shot Aubrey with a taser, then tied him to a pole in the bedroom and beat him. Carlos came to abduct her, steal her from Aubrey, and either kill or sell Drayton, the child that was not his. She looked at what happened from all angles to justify ramming her hat pin through his eye and causing him to seize. Nell nodded while Christaine talked, though killing was something she didn't like to think about because of her mother's murder. Nell told Christaine to go on; she wanted to hear how she justified killing Carlos.

"I looked at wild things, the lion pride. An outside male comes and kills the current male, and then kills all of the male's young. The female lions fight the new male for a while, but never win, and then they mate with him."

"So if Carlos had won, would you have gone with him?"

"Only long enough for him to turn his back so I could kill him again."

"I guess we're different than lions."

"But is that just social conditioning? What happened in primitive times with cave people?"

"Bet they acted like lions," Nell said.

"The other thing. When you mix your body fluids with someone to make a baby, are you related to that person now? You know, blood brother and sister? And if you kill him, is that some form of -cide, matricide, fratricide, or one of those -cides? Aubrey says his friend John Chrome goes around saying, 'You can't offend nature,' but you can, can't you? Did I kill some kind of family member when I did this to Carlos? Or is that acceptable because John Chrome is right, and you really can't offend nature? Is everything only natural?"

"I think I might kill him for what he did to you and Aubrey," Nell told her.

In her coma now, Christaine sees her father, Asante, come into the room like a ghost. He puts his hand on her forehead while she sleeps and prays to the Virgin Mary in Latin. *Ave Maria, gratia plena, Dominus tecum...* She sees his hands go around Carlo's throat as he prays. Then she is running in the dark again, the young girl, back to the shell pit where she left the altar boy mannequin to hold it and rock it in her arms until it all goes bad. A rattlesnake is there, swallowing Drayton, like the snake years ago in the back-yard at the old house, the one swallowing the squirrel while she and Aubrey watched. The snake turns into Carlos. She reaches for her belt like before and finds the long hat pin; the pin turns into a pistol. She shoots the rattlesnake into pieces, and the pieces turn into pieces of Carlos, dead on the ground.

In her hospital room, Aubrey sits. Her body is still, and he summons Triple Suiter.

"Is she gonna die, Trip? Is her brain hurt that bad or something worse?"

"There is a way I can find out. I will have to leave you to do it."

"Do it. How can I help?"

"You must put your face very close to hers, and I will leave through your nose into hers, then go to her brain and see what is."

Aubrey stood from the chair, bent down, and kissed her. Trip moved to where he wanted to go. Once in her brain, Trip sat for a moment, thinking about where to find her. "In the unlocatable location of things thought about, that's where she will be," he said under his breath. Another slipper came that lived there.

"Triple Suiter," the slipper said.

"I am. And you, you are Trista. I haven't seen or talked to you since I wrote the first Shallcross book, that whole group of us, slippers in a long meeting, sitting together in a circle in Aubrey's head. It was a miracle you were all able to leave your hosts and be there with me, and another miracle you were all able to get back to your hosts."

"Ah, but to sit together and tell those stories about our people. 'Mansion,' as Aubrey likes to say. It was all worth it. I heard you and him talking a minute ago in the hospital room, and I was expecting you."

"It is a visit. Are you alone in here with Christaine? Are there other slippers here?"

"The only other one is Juan, who was with us at the Shallcross meeting."

"Yes, Juan, the slipper who lived in Carlos's head. If I had not been able to talk to him about Carlos's life, then large parts of the Shallcross book would have been missing. Juan even kept a journal about his life with Carlos, and he gave it to me. Said he didn't want to think or be reminded of it anymore."

"When Juan came here two years ago, on the night Carlos assaulted everyone, he was a mess," Trista said. "We all were. It was just before Christaine pushed her hatpin into Carlos's eye, and Juan left him through his nose and entered hers. He was very upset he couldn't help Carlos as a person and had to give up. After our meeting with you in Aubrey's head, Juan and I came back here to Christaine, and he left me a note the next day, saying he had gone up into the mountains, her cerebral hemispheres, places in the brain as vast as the Andes and the Amazon on a microscopic level, as you well know. I haven't seen him for two years now."

"Trista, I would love to sit and talk about Aubrey and Christaine, who are much in love. I know you and I have lived their lives together, and we have lived their lives before they met, but I am here at Aubrey's insistence. He is so worried. Can I talk to Christaine, to her consciousness?"

"You are right, this is not the time for you and me to talk. I've just come from the area of bleed in the back of her head. Wait here. I will go and tell her light to come back to you."

Trip waited, as if he had just been let into the foyer of a Victorian house by the butler. Christaine's light came.

"Hello. I finally meet you," she said. "I've heard Aubrey say your name many times when he thought I wasn't listening."

"Yes, and it is an honor to meet you. Aubrey is so worried, and now that I am here, there are many things you need to know about Aubrey and me and his life so you can see how completely devoted he is to you."

"Yes. You can feel the movement on the outside, can't you? It's the hospital. I'm being moved. They're taking me to surgery to drill a hole in my skull to relieve the pressure. But that won't bother us, will it, Triple Suiter?"

"No, I would think not. Christaine, he so wants you to know everything about him, and he feels bad he hasn't found a proper way to tell you. The story is one that, as unlikely as it sounds, has been completely recorded, and while you are in this state on the outside from your injury, I can read you the story from a book named for him, then you will know everything he wants you to know."

"A book?"

Trip spun out a hologram of the old Florida hometown and its downtown area. Together, they stood at the entrance of a bookstore that had been shuttered a long time ago. Trip unlocked the door. There was enough light to see the tables and shelves of dust-covered inventory. Still upright in its metal display was the book, the five-by-nine copy of *Shallcross: The Blindspot Cathedral*. Christaine was like a child who'd seen a baby animal. She studied the cover, the artist's picture of two giant hands around the little dressage horse, the precarious large egg sitting in the saddle on its back. One of the hands held a hat pin like hers between the thumb and forefinger, the long pin she always carried between the leather layers of her belt like her father had taught her and her sister Marla to do for their protection. The pin on the book cover was pointed as if at any moment, it would prick the bubble in the picture, burst it, and allow the egg to fall from the horse's back and break.

"It's like life and everything is in this book cover," she said to

Trip. "Fragile. Balanced."

"Bird on a wire," Trip answered. "This is the part where we sit in chairs by the table over here, and I read the book to you so you will know everything Aubrey wants you to know." Trip began.

Aubrey...The Blue Goose...Trip...voice hearing...compulsions... swallowing...Trip...Aubrey's House...Joy.   Johnny Yuma...Punky...The Junior...Reve...the Shell Rock Road...the Catheter Café...Joy.   The toadstone ring...the Tower...blackouts...the Blind Spot Cathedral...Catholicism...Christaine Joy. Deaths...horses...the music...Joy.   The band...the rattlesnake... Drayton...Joy.   Carlos...the hat pin...Carlos's assault... death... Aubrey and Christaine...new life and a child...Joy.

He read to her all day and some of the night. They could hear the surgeon's drill on the outside. Henry Brown worked to release the blue-black blood on Christaine's brain. Occasionally, the whole bookstore rattled and vibrated from what they were doing to her skull, adding a shivaree of sound effects to the story. Trip read on. And when they felt her body being moved after surgery, they still kept going with the book, Christaine stopping him now and then to ask questions. Trip explained the world of slippers, of figurines, the world of voice hearers and bicameral minds that some were born with that hear the voices of souls belonging to the democracy of the dead, voices other people call schizophrenia.

When they finished the book, Trip said, "You have now heard the book of Shallcross. So what do you think of your Aubrey and all this?"

"Mansion, as he would say. Because it is, this story, and so are you, Triple Suiter."

"You're kind."

"Why can't I talk to my own slipper, Trista, when I wake up as the conscious Christaine? I have never done that."

"Maybe you can, even when you are not unconscious anymore. It's usually easy for someone to talk to us in the state you're in now, or a dream, unless you are born with the anatomy I explained, like Aubrey's. But maybe, who knows, you can after this."

"There is another book on the table called *Flame Vine*. It has the same name on it. Charles Porter. Who is that?"

"It is a pseudonym. It is Aubrey, and me. We are Charles Porter, three in one. Trinity stuff. But Aubrey doesn't want you to read the *Flame Vine* book just yet. Even Aubrey hasn't read that book. He's lived most of it but hasn't read it. Remember, you and Aubrey had an agreement not to talk about your past in detail and his past is in *Flame Vine*. You know, what he and John Chrome call the 'back peal'."

"Will I, as Christaine, remember this if I wake up from this coma?"

"Yes, all of it. It will be as clear as anything you have ever remembered, I promise."

"Where will you go next?"

"I told Aubrey to come back tonight. When he leans over to kiss you, he knows I will be waiting to move back to him through your breath."

Trip and Christaine left the building downtown. Outside, on the dreamscape street, Christaine turned and looked at the sign over the old store one more time. It read "Sonny's Book Store," then Trip dissolved the hologram he had made of the past.

She was still asleep. It had been four days. Her parents had a hotel room next to Aubrey's across the street and kept an eye on Drayton when Aubrey was with Christaine. John Chrome drove down every other night, then drove back to his teaching job. He was a good friend.

Leda and Arquette were trying to get up the nerve to reconnect with Aubrey while he was in Miami. On the fifth day, Aubrey was sitting beside Christaine's bed. Triple Suiter had told him about reading the book to Christaine inside Sonny's old place. She started to show signs of waking up. Dr. Brown was paged, and by the time he got there, Aubrey was bent over, hugging her, and they were talking.

"Well, well, good morning. I bet that's that longest night's sleep you have ever had," Brown said to her.

Her parents came. Drayton stood next to the bed and put his head on his mother's IV taped arm. She started crying. Aubrey left for the cafeteria to get her a cinnamon roll, and there they sat in the food court. Leda and Arquette.

Arquette and Aubrey tried to act manly and composed, shook hands, all that. Leda asked about Christaine; she could see Aubrey was joyous. The two men talked some, and Leda said, "Eleven o'clock. We should meet here every morning. We all had too much as friends to throw this away." Arquette looked at Aubrey and they half nod to each other. Leda walked down the hall.

They did meet the next day and the next day. Aubrey told Christaine what happened at the cafeteria, and she was not jealous of Leda. She listened to Aubrey's thoughts about his marriage when the *Shallcross* book was read to her, and she knew where Aubrey stood on all that. She told him about Triple Suiter, and the ground they covered in Sonny's bookstore. She described the store to Aubrey, a place he knew she had never seen, and the description was perfectly correct. He started crying in his hands beside her bed and asked now that she knew all this, would she leave him for keeping the voice hearing from her? Did she think he was too crazy to be around?

She said, "It was the only way I could have completely understood you and all of it – Triple Suiter coming to me in this coma and reading the book. Crazy?" She said she always knew he was and

177

made him promise to never change, then she told him to bring Leda and Arquette to her room. She wanted to meet them.

Christaine was in the hospital for a few more days. The other area in her brain that looked suspicious, the doctors thought was benign, congenital tissue. She told Aubrey she bet that was the house in her head where her own slipper Trista lived, visible on x-ray.

She was strong enough to go to the cafeteria in the mornings and sit with the long-estranged, half-patched-up group. One morning, when John Chrome was there, they were all laughing so hard about fate and bullshit they decided to do an impromptu batch of "Oh, yeahs," from the movie *Seven Beauties* to entertain Christaine, something they used to do in the old days before they knew her to entertain themselves, sitting half-drunk around a table in The Blue Goose.

Leda: "For the ones who think they live in the real world instead of Fort America. Oh, yeah."

Aubrey: "For the ones who dress well but have a single yellow tooth in front. Oh, yeah."

John Chrome: "For those who think the Jake brake is the sound of coming down. Oh, yeah."

Arquette: "For those who are vegetarian, and still feel like shit. Oh, yeah."

Christaine: "For those who think getting hit by lightning will make you a tree-top lover. Oh, yeah."

When she said that, she looked at Leda. Leda smiled and nodded, no umbrage in the room amongst them, it seemed. In unison, for the director of *Seven Beauties*, they counted one, two, three, and said extra-loud, "God bless you, Lena Wertmuller."

The next day, they met again, and Leda told the group about the patient in the hospital with the word MIDGE tattooed on his arm, and what he told Leda it meant.

"I'm telling you, that man Sonny had the same word tattooed on him, on his forearm. I saw it when I was in the bookstore."

When Aubrey was alone with Christaine, she asked if it was the same bookstore she was in with Triple Suiter. He told her it was, but it was closed and gone now, and Sonny was legally dead, according to Nell Kitching's lawyers.

"Then, when I was there with Triple Suiter, I guess it wasn't a dream. It was some kind of time travel. Is that right?"

"Yes. Something like that was being toggled, I think. Trip made you a hologram of it, I bet. He can do things like that from his side. The store was there for years, and what you heard him reading to you was true, stretched a little sometimes, but mainly true. You have to understand that what happened to you in the coma with my Triple Suiter is so credible to me because of the way I am."

"I love this thing. I had no idea about all this with you and him and your history in the town. How did you juggle that life and still function in the life you've led?"

"I only was worried it would drive *you* away from me if you knew I was like this. I don't care about anything or anybody else."

"And now I do know. I mean, I really know after that book was read to me. Something seemingly un-write-able, but I saw the actual book and heard its voice in the store, Sonny's store. Aubrey! The store downtown!"

"What?"

"Remember when Deputy Kimmel came to the house to ask questions about the twins who died months ago, Shane and Lane? The veterinarian and the alligator attack?"

"Of course."

"The store downtown, Aubrey. The deputy said Shane Richards told the vet the man burying the refrigerator with the body in it owned a store downtown."

"I know."

"And Aubrey, the story Leda told us yesterday about the tattoo on Sonny's arm is starting to all make sense."

Aubrey looked at her and chewed the inside of his cheek flesh. "The detailed account, I'm told – and the answer to the mystery – is in a book called *Flame Vine*, Christaine."

"I saw that book on the table in the store, but Triple Suiter said you didn't want him to read it to me."

"That's because I'm not supposed to read it, either. Trip won't let me. Says it violates some cosmic rule about the future or the past. Trip's not supposed to talk about those things. He says he's already broken some rules lately. And it's because you and I told each other, when we first fell in love, that we weren't going to go over our past, and a lot of my past is in that book. I had a wife, you had a husband, and now you and I have met them both, but that's all I want to know that's personal. Everyone has a history. I don't believe in the dredge, the dragline. I don't believe in hauling that stuff up through what we have now, don't you agree? That's what Trip calls 'fingering the finery.'"

"Yes. But that doesn't mean I can't crank up my best objective state and read that book one day."

"No problem. Just go for a ride in another thunderstorm and fall into a coma. I'll get Trip to show up in your head and read it to you, then you get a copy and read it to me. By the way, you meeting my ex sure went a lot smoother than when I met yours. The bastard tasered me in my own living room before we could be introduced."

"Don't, Aubrey. I can't even think about it. I can't believe how calm I stayed when Trip read that part to me. The stuff that was going through your mind when you were tied to the pole in the bedroom that night, the word palindrome you and Trip kept reciting to stay strong. 'You can cage a swallow can't you, but you can't swallow a cage can you.'"

"The word palindrome, yes. You can say it backward. Says the same thing. And it helped that night. I learned to swallow the cage. To deal with it."

"And then after it was over and you were in the hospital, you used the brain testing machine Dr. Brown had to take you back through it all. How could you do that? Isn't that what you'd call the dredge, the dragline?"

"I had to. It's asshole male, 'face your demon' shit, and that Nietzsche stuff. 'What doesn't destroy you makes you stronger.' But even that's dicey, because sometimes what doesn't destroy makes you weaker. I'm still more worried about you after that horror than me."

"Back to Sonny. What if Leda is right? What if it all tics into the man burying the refrigerator the Richards twins saw – the tattoo, the Freon huffing, the store downtown? What if it's one pot of clues pointing to the Tin Snip Killer?"

"The Tin Snip Killer? He was awful, Christaine."

Chapter 25: MORE STORIES

"This is the tale of two alligators, The Dragon and Two-Toed Tom. All the people thought they were bad gators and only hurt things around them, but they did many good things. Get in bed and pull the covers up. What are you wearing on your feet? Rabbits?"

"Animal slippers. Mommy bought me animal slippers. This one is named Tree Frog, and this one is named Triple Suiter."

"Oh, perfect, just perfect!"

"Tell me the story, Daddy."

"Okay. In the spring, when the wetlands and Everglades begin to dry up, The Dragon and Two-Toed moved from pond to pond, digging holes in the bottoms so the ground water would come back and the fish could live. People call these gator holes.

"One time, the two gators were swimming in the South Fork and saved a baby manatee from a bull shark. Between them, they tore the shark to pieces, and the manatee mother thanked them for saving her baby's life.

"Another time, Captain Nemo and Osceola guided their gators into the Everglades for a python hunt. The pythons came when Hurricane Andrew blew them from the pet stores in Homestead into the Glades. There they became big snakes and started killing all the furry animals."

"I'm gonna take my gator on a python hunt, Daddy." Drayton jumped off the bed and stood on his stuffed alligator like Freddie Tommie, then rolled it over in a deadly battle with a constrictor. Aubrey got down on the floor with him and made struggle and grimace noises, shouting, "Get hold of the snake's head, Drayton. I got his tail." Christaine heard them shouting downstairs and smiled. It was good. They both worried about their child after the accident and the emergency room.

"Okay, this python has worn me out. Time to get back in bed and sleep."

"But I wanna kill a bull shark next, Daddy."

"Tomorrow night. Those bull sharks will be sorry they ever came up the creek from the ocean. We'll get em."

"Promise."

"Yep. Turn the page. Slip away. Finished."

Chapter 26: BUSH HOG

A man stands in a place south of town, the Coconut Bar. A man the working class knows by the nickname Bush Hog. He mows rural property for a living with one. He does not belong to the good people. He is a cankerworm, striped mean, red and wrong from somewhere.

Bush Hog and Dan somebody were drinking with Claddy Nelson. Freddie Tommie worked for Claddy in the mowing and tree business now and then. Claddy bragged how his man Freddie could kill Brazilian peppers with a kind of Seminole hoo-doo he carried in a pouch. Bush Hog got the idea he could make a fortune if he could get hold of that and began to track Freddie. Showed up on Claddy's jobsites to shoot the shit about nothing, looking at Freddic and Freddie's compass. He and Dan thought of a plan to ambush him. Steal the pouch with the medicine in it.

One day, Freddie went to the secret place on the creek to see The Dragon and Two-Toed Tom. He knew Nemo and Osceola would have them lying in the sun because a cold snap had come through. That part of the creek was inaccessible and quiet, a hide out, and Freddie watched to see if he was followed. Bush Hog and Dan stayed way behind Freddie's truck, out of sight.

When Freddie approached the water after walking a mile through the scrub, he stopped and listened to all the sounds. He sat down low and waited to see if the sounds were normal. When he thought they were, he whistled a quail call. The coach whip came and circled him so fast Freddie couldn't turn his head quick enough to stay with him. Then the armadillo was there, rooting in the ground, acting oblivious to Freddie's presence, just like an armadillo. Freddie knew they were half blind, those creatures; he smiled as it tore holes in the ground with its bone snout, snorting like a pig.

Freddie stood and walked further down toward the creek, comfortable because he had seen the snake and the incessant rooter. The snake and Martha left ahead of him to tell the gators and slippers Freddie was there. Just as Freddie got to the water, Bush Hog put a gun in his back. Off to his left stood Dan with *his* gun.

"Well, look here, Dan. We done out-sneaked a great sneaker. Looks like we the real Indians today, and we got us ole Freddie here."

Freddie turned his head to Bush Hog. "This is a joke, Bush Hog, yes?"

"Oh, that'd be nice for you, Freddie, but not today. It's the cold call conundrum come on ya. I want to know everything about how you kill them pepper trees and what's in the little bag you carry around, that Indian magic or whatever. Lemme look at it."

"Not here. The bag's not on me. Not here."

"All right then, tell me what it is, where it is, and how you do it."

"It is private. Yes? It belongs to my world and the people who live in it. The human beings we are called by Dustin Hoffman in the movie *Little Big Man*," Freddie said, getting sarcastic.

"You tryin to be cute? I ain't got time to listen to no Indian movie bullshit. You ain't all Indian, anyway. I can see you some kinda blue gum; got nigger blood in you. Now quit looking at me and turn your head back around to the front." When he did, Bush Hog hit him with the butt of his shotgun. It stunned him, and they tied him to a tree.

The two men did not see the gators on the far bank, and the gators did not see them until Martha tapped them awake from the eyes of her coach whip and warned them. Nemo and Osceola slid the big bodies down in the water and moved closer to what was happening. Freddie came to, and Bush Hog kneeled beside him.

"What's in the bag that kills the pepper trees?"

Freddie just stared straight ahead and said nothing. Bush Hog pulled his knife, put the tip in one of Freddie nostrils, and slit it like Polanski did to Nicholson in *China Town*.

"How you like that movie, Freddie? I seen that one."

Bush Hog stood up again. "You ain't doin you no favors by gettin all tight-lipped on me, boyeh. I'll untie one of your hands and let you wipe your messed-up nose if you start talking to me about the stuff in the bag. Where is the bag?"

Freddie nodded to buy time. "In my truck, parked up the road, but it's hidden where no one can find it. Untie me, and I'll show you."

"Horse feathers! Don't you untie that animal, Bush Hog," Dan said. "Make him tell you where it is right here."

Bush Hog untied one hand anyway and left the other tied to the trcc. "Now wipe your nose and tell me, god damn it."

Freddie wiped his nose and threw the blood and snot at Bush Hog.

"See? I told you. You can't trust one a-these fuckin maroons, or whatever he is," Dan yelled at Bush Hog. "Now you got nigger Indian snot all over you. Gonna catch some kinda African shit."

Bush Hog fumed. He took a step toward Freddie. Cocked his shotgun. "I'm gonna shoot one of your feet off with a twelve-gauge bomb."

"Wait, wait, wait! You do that, no tellin who might hear it, Bush Hog. Let's gag him and cut on him some more. He'll talk," Dan said.

By now, Martha had her coach whip within ten feet of Bush Hog, behind some palmetto fronds. Two-Toed had inched his way towards the bank through the cattails to the same distance. The blind-acting armadillo came rooting away as a distraction, right between Bush Hog and Dan, like nobody existed. Dan saw it and kicked it, rolling it over. Bush Hog looked at the armadillo for a second. When Dan went to kick it again, Martha sent her coach whip up Bush Hog's loose pant leg. The snake went through the side of the man's underwear and put its head three inches into Bush Hog's rectum, the feeling famously like no other. Bush Hog dropped his shotgun and reached for his butt, screaming, "Oh! Oh! Oh!"

Dan was distracted for the three seconds it took Two-Toed Tom to rear up out of the shallow water on his tail and fall on him. Two-Toed seized hold of Dan's torso, shook him like a rat dog and simultaneously nailed Bush Hog with his tail, knocking him to the ground. Bush Hog, more concerned with where Martha's coach whip was, rolled around in the dirt. Two-Toed dropped Dan and went for Bush Hog. After a struggle, he got Bush Hog's head in his mouth. Bush Hog grabbed Tom's jaws, trying to pry them open, screaming, "No!" The gator's wide tongue muffled the sounds until Tom bit through, and then silence.

Tom carried Bush Hog's head over to Dan, who was dead twice over from the crush of twelve hundred pounds of gator. The Dragon bit through the rope holding Freddie's hand and freed him. All was quiet, and the friends sat there, breathing the fight out of them for a few minutes, until they were back to normal.

The animals moved closer to Freddie.

Nemo: "Well, this is an unexpected mess."

Osceola: "I'll take the heads."

Martha: "And the bodies?"

Osceola: "Leave them."

Nemo: "We can't leave them. This is too many kills. Let's hide them, or the county people will kill every alligator they can."

Osceola: "I'll move the bodies and heads to Tom's den up under the bank. Use it as a food supply for our gators."

Martha: "I agree."

Nemo: "Agree."

Freddie stood and looked at the sky. He began to chant, thanking his *Yaholi* and the Breath Master for saving him by sending him the animals of the forest and the water.

Chapter 27: THE INDIANS

It was the first quarter of moon in the month of June, the time of year for the Green Corn Dance, the *Shot-Catcaw*, it is called. The dance and annual meeting had slowly come back into favor with the tribe after dying down over the last fifty years. The Seminoles were trying to get their history back from the Christianity and modernism that had entered their culture, but they believed the two could coexist. The old beliefs were very important to them now. The visions were returning. Someone in the tribe said they had seen the *allapatta*, Billie Monday, walk out of a lake as an alligator, then turn into a man.

After Bush Hog and Dan's disappearance, Freddie told his employer, Claddy Nelson, that he was going to be a lot busier with his tractor and mowing service, though Claddy had no idea what he meant. Freddie did not tell Aubrey what happened with Bush Hog to protect him from being an accessory; he had told Aubrey months ago that he would do the killing. Bush Hog's mowing equipment sat idle on his place while he and Dan rotted up under Tom's hollowed-out arcade along the creek. Occasionally, the two gators fed on their putrid flesh like we do smoked fish. Bush Hog's ex-wife filed a missing person's report with the sheriff. Dan lived in an old trailer on the place and had no one.

Freddie and his son Yuchee came to Aubrey's on Saturday. Their little boys screamed and squealed, running around the yard. The grown-ups sat on the porch.

Freddie cleared his throat. "I came by to say hello, yes? Also, to invite you and Christaine to the Green Corn Dance west of the lake."

"When is it?" Aubrey asked.

"A week away. Next Saturday. Starts early. I want to invite

Nell Kitching, yes?"

"She'd love it, I'm sure. You don't have to ask me. Ask her."

"I will go up the shell rock road now to see if she'll come."

They were all in the truck at five AM. Drayton was staying with his grandparents and was not happy he couldn't go. Christaine said it would be too hard to keep track of him around a scene like that, and besides, Yuchee was not going to be there, either; his mother didn't want to see Freddie.

They left with Nell sitting in the back seat trying to stay awake, drinking her coffee after she took her morning meds. The sun came up behind them through cow country and hit the top of the Herbert Hoover Dike surrounding Lake Okeechobee, the liquid heart of Florida. The high dike was the cause of the lake's congestive heart failure – too much fluid trapped inside. That edema kept it from feeding and filtering its body, the Everglades, after being contained artificially in the lake for the last seventy years, unable to send enough water south through its grass kidneys to be processed on its way to the Gulf of Mexico. Now the Glades were drying up, dialysis was failing, and the chemical makeup was changing and poisoning the great *Pa-Hay-Okee*, or grassy waters, the Seminoles called it.

On the grounds of the reservation, the fires burned, the drums beat, and the dance started. Freddie took them to a chickee for introductions to tribe members, a palmetto frond thatched roof shelter made of cypress pole frames. He took Nell aside and told her that today she would get to meet his friend the medicine man, the one he promised her. Nell and Freddie walked off alone. Aubrey and Christaine went to watch the dancing.

About an hour into the day, Aubrey told Christaine he'd brought two tabs of MDA with him. She said he was crazy, but she was smiling when she said it.

"What are you thinking, Head Wound?"

"I'm thinking you've been out of the hospital for a while now, and you've got a head wound, too. But why not? We're fixed."

"I have to call my doctor in Miami and see if it's okay."

"Yeah, sure. See if you can get me a pass too."

They ate the drug, the Seminoles drank the magic black tea, and all of it seemed fitting for what was taking place.

Aubrey told her to try to be quiet for an hour, even though she would have the urge to talk and join the dance. "Just sit and fight it until you feel everything smooth out." By late morning, they were just right. By late morning, they thought what they had done was perfect for where they were today.

Christaine lit a cigarette and stared at Aubrey. She went through the smoking moves she knew he liked. Sometimes she held it in for a long time, slowly letting it out, never taking her eyes off him. When she lit a new one, she played out the oral thing, touching it with her tongue, picking something off her mouth that wasn't there, and shaping her mouth in exaggeration with the look of a woman on a man.

"If you keep doing that, we are going to have to walk off in the woods."

"Okay." She shaped her mouth that way again.

Freddie came over with Nell. "Do you want to taste the *sofkee* we make?"

They ate the starchy gruel served from a large black pot sitting over a low fire. They drank Cokes while the drums beat, and the dance went on.

Freddie saw that Aubrey and Christaine were in a state of grace. He took them to another chickee and told them it was okay to rest there. He said the chickee belonged to his mother's family; they could lie down out of the sun. He and Nell, who looked very awake from black tea, walked away again; when they came back, Freddie had a gopher tortoise in his hands. "These are special to us, and that man Sermon, with the building project, has buried a whole area of them alive. He bought permits from the state to do this. It is a crime what he did, yes? It is a crime the state lets him buy his way out. He offended nature."

"We'll get him, Freddie. The House will get him," Aubrey said.

Freddie nodded. He took Nell's hand and left toward the dance.

"What House are you talking about?" Christaine asked.

Because they had taken the MDA, and Trip had read *Shallcross* to her, he told her he was going to tell her lots of things today. "The House is an eco-warrior group. Want to join?"

"Sure, is there an initiation?"

"Nope, people like you, who have been struck by lightning and told about slippers in the holograms of secret books found in the holograms of abandoned bookstores, get an honorary membership."

"When's the next meeting?"

"In one hour. One hour, when I'm sure this drug will have prepared us like the black tea and the dance will have prepared the Seminoles."

"I think I'm right, right now."

Aubrey went into an explanation of what went on at the campsite – the appearances of the animals with the famous slippers inside them, and because of the *Shallcross* book, she both believed and understood what he was telling her.

Henry, the taxidermist, walked up. "What it is, Shallcross?"

"What it was, Henry."

"And what it shall be, Shallcross."

"This is Christaine."

"Yeah, I know. The woman named after Christ Jesus and the blood stains on him. The Junior told me."

"Hello, Henry," was all Christaine said.

"Okay, well, I gotta go see the head man over by the dance, Head Wound. Nice to finally meet you, Christaine." Christaine nodded, and Henry walked away.

"Kinda weird, huh?" she said.

"I know, he used that word 'finally,' cause he always thinks I don't come to see him enough."

They were high. Christaine was burning cigarette after cigarette. Aubrey was burning drifty after drifty. Nell came and took Christaine somewhere. Aubrey leaned back against one of the cypress poles in the chickee and went through his mind's foyer to the arcade in his brain where the congered tower in the middle of the cane field was. At the base was the Ball jar he always saw, the progenitor of shapes and hatcheries, floating waist-high next to the rope he used to circle the tower, the giant Eiffel he had mentally constructed years ago. It had been a while. Up on the rope and around the tower he flew, using the force of the turns to convolve and hatch, watching a toad stone smolder inside the Ball jar and taking great drags on the smoke through its top hole until he saw the Green Corn Dance in the glass, and all the famed dances of history – all the gambols and Terpsichorean flings he could remember: Zorba on the beach, dancing with the Englishman; he and Christaine's father, dancing in the round pen; Debra Kerr with Yul Brynner, the King of Siam; Patrick Swayze and the girl in the Catskills; Steve Martin, on the porch with the black people; Tom Petty and Mary Jane, last chance to kill the pain. Where were the Catholics and the dance? The Jews dance! They love to dance! How much more fun they must have had in Hebrew school while he sat in a stale catechism class. And his mother and father could dance. Oh, could they dance. All those World War II people could dance. They used to put his feet on top of theirs when he was small.

Triple Suiter dances! He'd seen him, dancing on fire, till the end.

Around the tower he spun, faster and faster, like Speedy in the Globe of Death, knowing it would get past a certain safe point and reliably it did. The Mess Hall was coming. He couldn't stop it. Now he saw people dancing on graves. He was on a highway in his truck, moving, moving past people holding hands. "*Hava nagi-la*," they sang, dancing around Stars of David, around station after station of road kill cross – crosses with flowers, deflated balloons, rotting teddy bears, votive candles, and copy machine photographs hanging off them instead of Jesus. He had gone too far. Wanted to put it through the blades of his Ball jar, tip it up, and drink it, swallow it, so he could know it when it got slim enough to go down, until the shudder, the frisson, and the impossible valedictory song showed, "DID YOU COME BY AGAIN, TO DIE AGAIN? WELL, TRY AGAIN, ANOTHER TIME."

"My god. Stop it. He's coming!" Trip screamed at him inside. "One Mississippi, two Mississippi…" The Slim Hand counted and crammed the huge black pot of *sofkee* cooking in the chickee down his throat. He started to spasm.

"Start the rhyme! Start it!" Trip yelled.

"WHEN YOU CAN'T SEE, TAKE A STRAIGHT SHOT

RIGHT THROUGH THE HEART OF THE BLIND SPOT,

TRUE MAGAZINE KNOWS THE TRUTH,

RIGHTY TIGHTY, LEFTY LOOSE!"

An Indian woman bent over him with two others. They put something under his head. He saw the jagged colored patterns in their tribal clothes. "Mister," one said, "you are full of spirits. This man here with us is sacred. He is our *allapatta*, our *yaholi*. He will help you to feel better."

Billie Monday kneeled. "Your name is Shallcross. Are the crosses and stars of Judah in your dream gone, the ones on the side of road? Has the demon you call the Slim Hand left you?" Aubrey looked incredibly in his eyes. A huge slipper exploded through the old man's iris, waving its hands in smoke trails, then disappeared.

Billie Monday whispered the same rhyme that he and Trip had just chanted together. When he finished the rhyme he said, "Sit up, son. I have been waiting for you."

Freddie, Nell, and Christaine were standing there too now, and Freddie was smiling. The medicine man stood. Said he had to go back and dance more. "Christaine told me you swallowed some religion," Freddie said to Aubrey. "This is the perfect place, yes?"

"For a minute, I wasn't so sure. I swallowed more than religion."

"Come on, let's go over by the dance," Freddie said.

"Christaine, come here, please. Are you all right?"

"I am. I am. What happened to you, Aubrey?"

"I was fine until my head turned over. I had one of my Slim Hand things. I went too far out around the tower. Do you remember all that about the tower from the *Shallcross* book?"

"Yes. Are you okay?"

"Yes. How come you're so okay?"

"Because we are different, my love. We are different."

"Tell me. Tell me, how are we different?"

"Oh, Aubrey. I do narration all day long. You do dialogue and Wonder Dog skits, you call them. You stage everything in a beautiful, but sometimes scary way. I understand now, since your Triple Suiter and I read the book. There's just one thing, though."

"What?"

"I'd give anything for a physical copy of that book."

"So would I."

"And oh, yes, something happened a minute ago you didn't see. Nell and I saw it, and I'm glad she was with me, or I might never have believed it. The two alligators from the House, as you call it, The Dragon and Two-Toed Tom, came out of the water by the village and a young Indian boy was sent forward by that old mystagogue, Billie Monday. The boy kissed each alligator on the head and hung a wreath of flame vine in bloom around their necks. When the alligators went back in the water, they both pushed up high on their tails for the crowd and then swam away. I think that's what I saw."

"You saw it. You saw it. It's true. I know this. It's true."

"Did you get what I said about the flame vine wreaths? I want to read that book, too, Aubrey! I want to read that other book in the bookstore about your life before I met you – *Flame Vine*."

Around the main fire, the tribe honored Henry for raising rattlesnakes, and Billie Monday praised him for teaching snail kites to hunt baby pythons. Billie presented Henry with a fulgurite, created when lightning struck the Florida sand and melted it into an abstract crystal, sometimes a foot long. Only the heavens and the white light of the tropics knew the meaning of this. Next, they honored Freddie for killing Brazilian pepper trees; the rest of what he had done, the other killings, was supposed to be a secret, but his people knew. Freddie stood in the middle of the circle while sand hill cranes and white ibis walked tame around him and the others there. Their oracle, Billie Monday, gave a speech about the invaders (he called them "the exotics") – plants and animals from other places. Some of the Indians couldn't help glancing at the whites present when he said it, but today one white was one of them – Henry, the rattlesnake keeper – and one Black Seminole was more than that, Freddie, the other powerful *allapatta*.

Chapter 28: SONNY

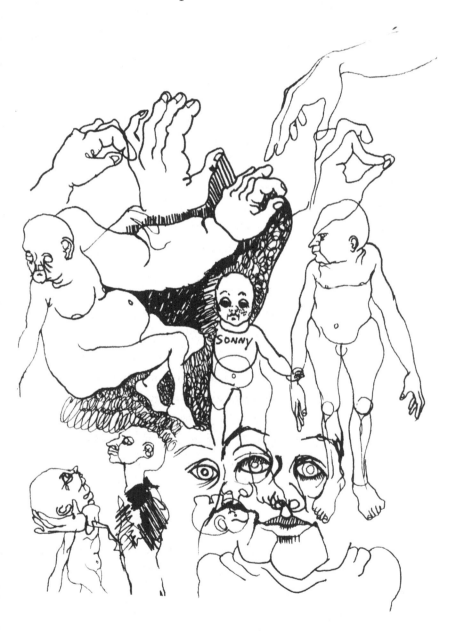

I've been thinking about Sonny and the bookstore, me,
Triple Suiter. The book, *Flame Vine*, still sits in its dusty display
stand there. It is a book about my life with Aubrey as a child and
as a young man.

Right before Sonny disappeared, I met his slipper Freegrace.
Freegrace had slipped to the girl Annie one night when Sonny was
in his last days as a human. Annie always waited on Sonny and
Aubrey at The Blue Goose. Freegrace went to Aubrey when Annie
leaned over close to Aubrey's face to put his food down on a ta-
ble. Freegrace spent time with me in Aubrey's head. He told me
Sonny's life story, a story I did not know. Sonny was twelve years
older than most of the Blue Goose bunch. In *this* story, *Animal
Slippers*, I've had to watch the group of friends try to figure out if
Sonny was the Tin Snip Killer.

Sonny lived alone with his crazy mother after he lost his father
in the war. Freegrace remembered Sonny as admired in high school
– a football player and president of his class, the class of 1950. That
year was the summer of ruin, the summer that cooked him.

He started hanging out with a boy who showed him how to huff
Freon from refrigerator compressors. Sonny would run through
town in his underwear when he was high. The police would cap-
ture him and take their football hero home. He caught leprosy in
one hand from the armadillos he ran down and handled to show
off for his girlfriend. Armadillos carry leprosy in their hind legs,
where the temperature is only ninety-three degrees and perfect for
the bacterium to live. Sonny was taken out of school and sent to a
leprosarium. He never got to graduate. When a new drug cured the
leprosy, he had missed a certain part of his life and his right hand
was deformed and so was he.

In the leprosarium, Sonny read lots of books, and in the craft
shop, he learned how to make a ship in bottle. He loved enclosed

things. He tried to imagine
what it would be like to put
his mother in a bottle so she
could never get out. When
he was eight years old, his
mother made a dummy with
a coconut head, using sea-
shells for buck teeth, and
named it Mortimer Snerd.
She would come at him with
the dummy, telling him the
dummy had a pair of snips
and was going to cut him into
strips and split his tongue if
he wasn't a good boy.

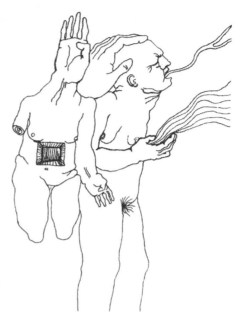

Sonny grew up to hate women his mother's age. If he thought
they were mean, especially to children, he knocked them unconscious, filled their lungs with Freon, and cut their skin into strips
with tin snips, like the ones his mother said her dummy had. He
placed their bodies in discarded refrigerators at dumpsites, the
doors left wide open, their last shape arranged and surrounded by
mayonnaise jars, electrical wire, broken toys, and other bilge from
the dump, things considered essential treatment for his creations
inside the white totems of Freon gas. He put them in there like
ships in bottles, holding Polaroid pictures of their murdered selves.
The paradox? He considered himself a vigilante and protector of
children and animals. At the same time, he hated himself for what
he was doing, but he couldn't stop.

ANIMAL SLIPPERS

Chapter 29: SONNY OR SERMON

Sonny or Sermon? Which one would be next? Arquette had called from Miami last night and said he was on his way to Jensen Beach. He wanted to look into all this talk about Sonny; it would give him and his anxiety a much-needed something to do. Henry the taxidermist used to say, "That boy Arquette is so uptight, he should take one a-them stool softeners every day."

Aubrey moped, complaining he was pulled in ten different directions. Christaine laughed at him, calling him "Poor little rich boy" – Aubrey and Arquette with their money and time. Aubrey kept saying to himself, "Arm and Hammer, Arm and Hammer," telling his body to get busy. Yes, work, like the Richards twins told him, the vaccination against depression. Work! the surefire distraction from the tortuous sound of the cicadas in the pine trees that doubled the pain of anyone mid-day doing nothing.

Christaine stayed out of the Sermon thing for now and chose instead to investigate the mystery of Sonny because of her friend Nell. She went to talk to Detective Kimmel, and he was happy she showed interest in the case.

"I've been working on this thing ever since I can remember. It's a fascinating series of crimes," Detective Kimmel said.

Christaine, formerly a reporter, searched microfilm for headlines and articles about the Tin Snip Killer in the local paper's archives:

Wednesday, February 22, 1954
Local Murdered

Children playing in the woods south of Stuart found Rebecca Kitching's body in a discarded refrigerator, allegedly stabbed to death. Sheriff Roy Baker said more details would be released after the coroner's investigation, and a...

Thursday, February 23, 1954
Kitching Murder: Coroner's Report

The coroner today said Rebecca Kitching, wife of Walter Kitching and mother of Nell Kitching, died of asphyxiation from Freon gas, a coolant in refrigerators. Wounds inflicted by a pair of tin snips were apparently caused post-mortem. It is unclear how she came into contact with the gas, but the sheriff's office has reached out to the FBI for input. A message on the door of the refrigerator, written in the blood of the victim, read, "Ship in a Bottle." The sheriff's office asks anyone with information about this crime to come forward and says...

Tuesday, June 28, 1966
Community on Edge from Another Tin Snip Killing

The body of Alice Grainger was found yesterday in a copy of a twelve-year-old murder. Sheriff Rex Green believes it could be the same person the press dubbed the Tin Snip Killer, or it could be a copycat. Tin snips were found at the scene, and the victim was holding a Polaroid of herself inside a discarded refrigerator. The sheriff's department found other similarities between the two killings. Today, there will be...

Saturday July 11, 1975
Man's Body Found in Hobe Sound's Community Park

A man's body was found Friday morning inside a refrigerator on the grounds of the community park, with many details mirroring the Tin Snip Killer murders. Officials revealed a striking difference in the murders today, in hopes the public may have information leading to the perpetrator. The message written in the victim's blood on the door read, "He Offended Nature."

While Christaine nosed around the Sonny question, Aubrey

and the House planned the next move on Sermon. As it turned out, they didn't have to do much. Sermon was coming apart. He'd heard about Vito dying of bath salts at the carnival. What would happen to Kong, the big chimpanzee he was so fond of? He would buy him. Yes, that's what he would do, and he would give him a good home. He had to find a way to make himself feel like a compassionate human being, to disabuse this great ape, who had been through so much. The next morning, he went to the winter quarters looking for the man Kong liked, the man who would enter the ring and stage a fight with Kong for the crowd; he was a man Sermon wanted to hire.

The man filled him in and told him to talk to Speedy and Roberta about buying Kong. They knew the show's owner in Ohio. Speedy wrote a phone number down and was short with Sermon. Sermon called the show office in Ohio, and Speedy called Aubrey to tell him what Sermon was up to. The owner of the show was dying to rid himself of the chimp and equipment and sold Kong and his steel living cage to Sermon for a catchpenny price. Sermon hired the man who staged the fake fights to help him get acquainted with the ape.

Sermon was beginning to experience certain vestibular disturbances – storms in the inner ear, the onset delamination of who he thought he was, a constipative feeling that he was all wrong inside squatted in his gut. Yesterday, he read an article in the Sunday paper, a retrospective on the Tin Snip Killer called "History of Our County." What ear-wormed Sermon was the description of the last killing in 1975, and the words written in blood on the refrigerator door that read, "He Offended Nature." Or maybe it was the languor of Sermon's everyday life getting to him from a poison meaninglessness. He had come to Florida to reinvent himself as a developer, get away from the crepehanging vitamin and smoothie charade, the

TV gadget grift, and be admired for building what he thought were beautiful Florida houses, even though their elevations and tectonics screamed ostentorium. He had no idea as he aged he would start to feel closer to his dog than his wife, who stayed up in Greensboro at the other house. They had no children. It sat on him.

He saw the advice on TV, he saw in his mail – what it did for the elision of loneliness and depression to have animals or a pet around, especially as you got older. There was a time he wouldn't swerve or brake for a squirrel in the road, but the other day, he almost wrecked to avoid one. These days, it was Kong that kept his mind off the grand jury investigation of his baldness cure. It was Kong, our relative, Sermon's adopted son, in a way, that had connected with Sermon's eyes night after night at the fights. Should he rename him or leave the show name on? He'd leave it; Kong's name would be an important prompt. People would ask, and he would tell Kong's story – how bad Kong's life had been, how interesting yet sad, made to slug it out with drunken men for money, and how God must have punished Vito his owner in the end with bath salts for perpetrating the whole thing. That's when Sermon sucked air one morning for something awful he had done and was having nightmares about.

The state of Florida at the time allowed a gratuity to be paid if a developer found the endangered gopher tortoise on his land. A developer could pay off the state, legally, and bury them alive instead of capturing them and relocating them at a greater expense. The developer also had the option to set aside an area of preserve for the turtles at an even greater personal expense. Such an area had once been allotted for tortoises as part of a project in Palm Beach County, where three hundred and twenty tortoises were found. It took one hundred and eighty-one acres of preserve to satisfy the state at a cost to the developer of a hundred thousand dollars per tortoise, but it was done.

In another case, Walmart built a store with five tortoise burrows on the land and paid $11,409 for a permit to bury them alive. Sermon had twenty-five burrows on his land. It cost $65,000 to bury them alive. He chose to pay that, rather than set aside land or relocate them. Five days ago, the turtles had been buried. They were under there, still alive, dying, and Sermon was beginning to get mental. When he lay down at night, he could see his dry heart form over a faucet, but the water wasn't running.

Freddie had shown a tortoise to the group at the Green Corn Dance and told them Sermon paid the state to bury them. The group, the House, was out for Sermon for doing this and needed to work fast.

Aubrey was weeding in the yard when he saw the coach whip fly by and come back to where he was. "They would like to see you at the creek tonight," Martha the Gypsy lady told him from the nose of the snake. He made arrangements and took the same mare to the campsite by the water. At 5:30 AM, the big gators began walking out of the water. The snake and the armadillo came from the woods. All of the slippers stood in front of the fire pit. Nemo spoke.

"We plan to make him suffer like the tortoise."

The next night, Freddie, carrying a large tortoise, moved through the woods as quiet as the long snake who followed him. What entry locks at Sermon's house the coach whip couldn't pick with its prehensile tongue, Martha had it picked with the stiff tip of its tail. No alarms went off, or maybe Sermon had forgotten to set them. He had been drinking a lot lately.

There in his king-size bed, his head back, mouth open, he slept. No dog. The wife had taken it with her three days ago to Greensboro. Freddie slipped the tortoise under the sheets a couple of feet from Sermon's legs and left. It took about five minutes for the tortoise to crawl into a leg. That was when the camera moved up and away from the house in this story for an aerial view. The southern angels in the clouds heard the screams below, the same ones we heard in *The Godfather* after the mafia put the severed horse head in bed with a man who had crossed them.

The next morning, Sermon was on the project at the tortoise burial site. He had been told the creatures could live two or three weeks without food or water. He ran around the sandy area, screaming at the workmen to bring the backhoes and use shovels and their hands when they got close to a covered tortoise burrow. Each turtle was found. Sermon held them one at a time and cried, as they were rescued. The rough workmen were laughing at a distance, shaking their heads, mumbling that he had lost it. The recovery had gone on all day stopping the project. Sermon was not satisfied until all were saved. He had turned on his old insensate self. He had changed.

That week, he contacted the Florida Fish and Wildlife Conservation Commission and began plans to set aside twenty acres for a preserve. His life and beliefs were making the shift. He had the workers build a temporary fenced-in area and fed lettuce to the turtles every day, standing at the fence talking to them, apologizing, while an informant who worked for Big Jim Lovill up in North Carolina sat on a bulldozer and watched.

Chapter 30: THE SEARCH PARTY

Nell had only seen the property she inherited from Sonny once, with her lawyer. The lawyer took his jeep because the dirt road into the two-acre lot was almost impassable – scrub, branches, deep sand.

The place where Sonny led his insular life was on the backwaters of the St. Lucie River, beside a creek called the South Fork, across from one of the many pastures of the immense Harris Ranch. The foreman of that ranch was Darnell Drinkard, whose mother Aubrey met at the local hospital before Christaine was transferred to Miami with her head injury. Yes, Mrs. Drinkard knew of Aubrey; told him she was there with her autistic son, whose nose had been broken. Said when her son was born, "An egg must have broke in his head," Aubrey remembered as he, Nell, Christaine, and Drayton turned down the jungle road to Nell's new inheritance.

"I think that's an old double wide under all those Brazilian pepper trees over there, Nell," Aubrey said.

"Spooky. This is spooky," Christaine said.

"Maybe. I liked Sonny. Sonny always came to see me when I was in the crazy place."

"You think he could have been the Tin Snip Killer?" Christaine asked.

"From what I've read about humanity, I guess any of us could, but I would hate to think he killed my mother."

"Some of the clues we've been researching could be coincidental, but I'm enjoying the rising action so far," Aubrey laughed. "You have a key to what's left of that trailer?"

"Don't need one. The place has already been broken into and trashed."

There were piles of old paperbacks, two tables, and large,

empty bottles in different sizes and colors.

"You think Sonny bought old books for his store and brought them here to patch them up on these tables, Nell?" Christaine asked.

"He did have a used book section, I remember."

Outside, they toed the junk around in the high grass on what was once an old lawn. Rotted wooden chairs, a rusted grill, and what was left of Sonny's ancient car, which was collapsed on its flat tires.

It was only about a hundred feet across the water to the mangroves on the other side of the creek. Aubrey saw debris washed up under the bowed-out roots of the trees and of course a six or seven foot long gator staring at him out in the water.

"Wish I had a john boat. I'd go over there and look at whatever that is."

"Where?"

"Against the bank."

"Trash, but whose trash?"

"Maybe something of Sonny's. Nice place in a way, though, Nell, and nice of him to leave it to you. He came to town with his mother. She worked in the dentist office we went to as kids."

"Yes. I thought she was kind of an unhappy woman."

"Shit, that woman used to tell me if I didn't brush my teeth correctly, they'd fall out, or I'd end up looking like Mortimer Snerd, Edgar Bergan's buck-toothed dummy. 'Up and down like this,' she'd say, 'or you miss the cracks, boy,' then she'd pinch the hell out of me. I was ten, and she was a specter in my bathroom mirror for years when I brushed, especially if I felt guilty about something I'd done. Sometimes I think I had to deal with her standing behind me more than the Catholic Church."

"Hey, look over here. Looks like something dug some holes," Christaine said.

"Armadillos did that."

"Not this one, Daddy," Drayton said, standing next to a small, deep hole.

"I bet that's where his septic tank is. Looks about right when you square it with the trailer, Drayton."

On the way home, they all gave their opinions about what should be done to the place – clean it up and sell it, or use it for a country place.

Aubrey kept thinking about the objects he saw on the other side of the creek. Two days later, he drove out to the Harris Ranch to get a look, since it was on their side of the water.

"Good morning. Is Mr. Drinkard here? I would like to speak with him if I could."

"I'm Mr. Drinkard, but just Darnell to you, Mr. Shallcross."

Aubrey laughed. "And I'm just Aubrey to you."

"I used to see you at all the rodeos when I was a teenager," Darnell said. "You was one good bareback bronc rider. How come I never seen you on saddle broncs?"

"See these legs a-mine? I couldn't spur saddle broncs like the short guys could, but these legs could stay out over those bareback horses' shoulders."

"And you were always with that big guy, Junior Nelson. He was a good bulldogger. Got a college scholarship to play football somewhere. It was awful, him gettin bit by that coral snake in the mouth. What a accident."

"Yeah, he was a good friend. I wonder if I could ask you a favor. A friend owns a small piece of land on the south side of the creek that borders the ranch. I wonder if I might go down there and look at that place from this side?"

"C'mon, let's jump in the truck. I'll take you."

They walked by two horse trailers. The side of one was torn out on the bottom. "Horse do that?" Aubrey asked.

"Naw, would you believe a gator did it?"

"A gator?"

"Not just any gator, if you can keep a secret."

"I'm good."

"I had that gator with two toes on one foot in there. Saw him in the big fill pond down about a mile from here, and I dropped a stick of dynamite in the water where he went down. Got him back to the house all stunned, but alive. Put him in the trailer tied out, and if I told you the rest, you gonna think I been smokin' whacky weed."

"Like I said, I'm good for it."

"Well, bout three in the morning, I got up to check on him, and there was that hole in the side of the stock trailer and two sets of gator tracks headed out the yard. I run after them on a horse with the dogs, but they got to the water first. Outrun me."

"What you mean, they? You tellin me another gator tore out the side of that horse trailer and got him out?"

"God's teeth, one did. I know. You think I'm crazy, but I got witnesses on horses next to me that night that saw two gators runnin together before they hit the water."

"No. I don't think you're crazy. I might even be one of those witnesses to support what you just told me."

Darnell looked at Aubrey and smiled, thinking Aubrey might be kidding him. They drove and stopped at a set of cow pens. Darnell got out and talked to the men for a few minutes, then came back to the truck. "My man Lester is comin with my brother on the halftrack shortly. They been huntin hogs this morning." Aubrey nodded. "I'm gonna take us down to this side of the creek in the halftrack the rest of the way, cause it's boggy down there. Okay with you?"

"Yeah. Haven't been on a halftrack in years."

"Just to let you know, my younger brother will be with us, and he's little bit gone-minded. He has autism, but he has gotten better at communicating."

"I met your mother Betty at the hospital not long ago, and we had a talk about all that. Nice lady."

"My little brother was friends with the man who owned that property you wanna see. He was always nice to him and gave him odd jobs around his place. My brother Dewey – we call him Half Track, cause he's so crazy to ride on mine – well, that boy would swim the damn creek, gators and all, to get over to that man's side. Never could remember the man's name."

"Sonny. His name was Sonny. Owned a small bookstore in town."

The men on the halftrack were all Florida cowboys in worn snap button shirts, belt buckles, and non-felt hats for the hot weather. When they got to the creek bank, Dewey got down and started pointing at Sonny's place on the other side.

"Sonny," he said a couple of times.

Aubrey walked to where the objects were and looked at them. There was a plastic mask and tangled plastic tubing. He put them in the garbage bag he brought. Half Track started to wade in the water, as if he was going to swim to the other side. He motioned to the others to come, too.

"Boyeh!" his brother shouted. "You come outta there right now. We ain't crossing that creek with you, and you ain't, either, gator bait." Half Track waded back.

That night, everyone – Nell, Arquette, Speedy, Roberta, and even John Chrome – came to Aubrey and Christaine's. The contents of the garbage bag from Sonny's were emptied on the porch table. There was a mask and plastic tubing that looked like something emphysema patients wore, along with latex gloves, rotted paper and the remains of an inhaler in the bottom of the bag which gave the friends no clues.

At his home, Sermon thought about changing his life. Kong had befriended him with the help of the man from the carnival. The great ape would even hold his hand now. Sermon's moral vestibule had been rocked by the advent of a new conscience, but he owed the bank and Big Jim, and needed his draws to get the project done. The whole mess was a mental fibroid to him; he was like a man having an affair on his wife, but the new mistress was from the world of *animale* instead of human, the world he had taken on like Prozac to feel better.

The body of the House, the slippers and their army, prepared to intervene again. Martha came to Aubrey's place with her armadillo this time to summon him. Drayton saw the armadillo first and chased it around the yard, then Aubrey recognized the creature and stopped him.

"Sorry bout the kid, Martha."

"Sweet Gypsy Jesus. Too bad I didn't bring my coach whip. I would have scared that kid to death with him."

"I don't know, Martha. He's got a knife, and he's gettin pretty good with it. What's up?"

"Tomorrow night, go to the creek."

He hobbled the mare in the field behind his camp. She was getting used to that, and she loved being able to graze all night.

"What's it going to be tonight, Trip, more James Taylor?" Aubrey asked as they waited for the group of slippers.

"Um, sweet baby Aubrey doesn't do it for me."

"Well, how bout we do some old stuff like we used to do in the Catheter Café, when Janet worked there?"

Trip came on with the sound of a record drop from the ancient 45 RPM turntables and started singing, "I Want You To Be My

Girl," by Frankie Lymon and the Teenagers. Then Trip did Little Anthony and the Imperials, like he always did when they ate breakfast in the old café. He and Aubrey dragged the song line back over the scene in the first Shallcross book that took place at Frankie Lymon's funeral after he overdosed – Frankie lying in a casket while famous doo-wop singers filed by to get their last look at the kid with the golden throat.

"Aw, it's just too bad you shot that dope, Frankie," Aubrey and Trip said in unison. "That ten-carat tenor of yours influenced some of the greats – The Temptations, Smokey Robinson, The Beach Boys."

"Yeah, how did you put it Trip?" Aubrey asked. "There lies Frankie in the pine box, kicked in the heart by a China white horse, at an age tragically too young to die. Good one, Mr. Suiter, good one."

"You think the fans would get the China white part?"

"Well, some. Some people know that's heroin."

They sang more from that era before Trip reminded him to take his Trazadone and wait for the voices he referred to lately as Lothar and the Hand People. "They will be coming as always to ask you to pick a film tonight, Aubrey."

"Yeah, right, Trip. They are the Hand People, and I be ole Lothar."

Aubrey went down to the Trazadone Lounge but veered off somewhere besides a movie and went right to sleep. He dreamed he was tiny again, like a slipper. He was with Martha in the eyes of the coach whip. They painted their faces black and wore tan clothing to look exactly like the snake.

Martha gave a signal, and the wire of scales took off at full speed along the pine needle ground, coursing through palmettos and myrtles, up a moraine and down into a depression in the ground where he surprised a wood rat, and the chase was on.

"I have to let him have it. Hold on," Martha said.

"Oh, no." Aubrey shook his head as they rocked back and forth in their seats, their necks straining from the G forces. The sand flew. The snake and the rat mixed turns with straight runs until the rat flipped from a spin-out, and the coach whip was there.

"It will take a little time for him to swallow the thing. We can sit and talk."

"Sure," Aubrey said.

"How do you think I look at my age? Fifty."

"Like a Gypsy woman with olive skin should – pretty damn good."

"Aubrey?"

"I do. It's tougher on us blond people, this aging thing."

"I was thinking of having plastic surgery," she said.

"What?"

"I have a boyfriend, you know. It's not that I want to last forever. It's just that I want it to last long enough so, when I do get old and he gets old, it will be easier for us to forgive each other."

The snake swallowed. They took off again, but a little slower with that lump in its body.

"You know that old saying about the light at the end of the tunnel, Martha?"

"Yes."

"To me that might mean the pharmaceutical companies."

Aubrey smiled and Martha laughed and laughed until it trailed off, and Aubrey opened his eyes at 5:30 in the morning. The House of all the animals had come from the water and the woods.

"My friends," Nemo said, dressed in his 19th-century best, with a top hat and a cravat for fascination, one would guess, "we should continue our efforts towards the common good. We must be paladins for the wild animals on this earth. Templars! Crusaders! There is a crisis. The animals are disappearing. We cannot let up on Sermon and the project, though the man is changing. He seems to be having a crisis of conscience, but let's not trust it. I want Martha and her snake to invade his house tomorrow night and bring him a dead cockade woodpecker from the trees he recently felled. That should more than spook him.

"If the environmental people had discovered endangered birds were on the project in the beginning, they would have cut Monsieur Sermon out of many more acres of land. It must be you, Martha. The alligators are hard to manage right now because it is breeding season, and every female Osceola and I run across wants to be courted by The Dragon and Two-Toed Tom. Osceola and I have been taken for some fast rides and passionate swims lately. So yes, Martha, I don't trust the alligator boys in this state. The season for making baby gators is almost over, but until then, you are going to have to do this to Sermon alone."

"I will, Captain. I will. Let the alligators live a little," she laughed.

"Aubrey, can you meet with the Sermon man and your lawyer? See if there is any accretion of weakness in his character from his recent behavior with the gopher tortoises at Cypress Prairie?"

Aubrey said he'd try.

Martha needed a dead woodpecker from the area to make her point. She began with her armadillo at the other end of the project, away from the woodpecker carnage. She stood the armadillo on his hind legs and watched his right front leg extend, his toenails unfurled, then pop! A spark flew out from between them into the dry grass, and the fire was on. W-h-i-n-e. She heard the batteries powering the security guard's golf cart, headed for the spot.

Martha sent the armadillo into the woods to hide and switched to her snake. Sitting inside the snake's eyes in her high speed safety chair, with the snake's black head the usual eight inches off the ground, she flew through the woods, telling him where to go around palmettos and pine trees until they reached the sand ridge close to the newly created gopher habitat. From there she took the snake way over to the left, where the downed shortleaf pines on the high ground were in piles.

"There," she told her snake. "Now use your nose and find me a bird corpse."

It took a half hour before the snake got into a place where the body of a red cockade was tucked up under a tree. "Now we say a few words of prayer, put our nose close to the bird, and see if a slipper survives in its body." There was. His name was Fred. She took him on board the snake. He told Martha he'd thought he might have to move to something as low as the worms eating the bird, until she found him. Martha nodded and told Fred he owed her a favor, like a good Gypsy woman would. "Now, hold on and get ready for the ride. After you've been in the saloon of a coach whip's eye while it runs the woods, you will not want to ever live in another bird."

They took off, the snake carrying the body of the dead cockade in its mouth. Martha became concerned about the size of the job, taking the dead woodpecker over to Sermon's house and wanted help. She talked to Nemo. Nemo had The Dragon carry her across the river to Aubrey's, where Martha asked him to arrange a meeting with Speedy and Roberta. The meeting turned emotional for everyone when Roberta saw the snake. Roberta and Martha both cried. The coach whip was the same one Speedy threw in the woods when he was mad at Roberta, and Speedy apologized over and over.

The next night on his motorcycle, Speedy took Martha, her coach whip, and Roberta's coach whip piloted by Roy, in the saddlebags to the gates of the posh development where Sermon lived. Inside the compound, the two snakes slid through the fence, found the house, and easily carried the dead woodpecker inside. Before Martha put the dead bird in Sermon's bed, she and Roy performed much mischief to further derange Sermon's head. The two snakes' capabilities were endless. Not only could they pick locks and open doors, but they could squeeze through anything, open jars, and drag stuff across a room together. They were eight feet long and strong. The snakes invaded silverware drawers and put knives, forks, and spoons in the oven, as if they belonged there. They quietly moved furniture around. Martha was satisfied that the mix would upset the developer when he found it.

Last, she and Roy had the snakes take the red cockade's eyeless body, ants still moving inside the sockets, to Sermon's bed and leave it by his face on the pillow.

In the morning, the camera moved up high and away from the house again for all of us. It became the same aerial shot as the morning Sermon found the big gopher turtle in his bed. You could hear the sowing wails of the man when he woke and couldn't move, looking into the face of a rotting, ant-filled bird, giving a whole new meaning to "still life with woodpecker."

ANIMAL SLIPPERS

Chapter 31: BIG JIM LOVILL

When Big Jim got up in the morning, he turned on the TV. He liked to play with the pause button on the channel changer and stop faces in mid-expression so he could study them, looking for pantomimes he could practice his lie detector hobby on. Big Jim learned to read faces from his mother Betty Mae, and she learned from her mother, rumored to be a Scottish witch. It had been very useful to him. He was also half-raised by a wise black woman who nursed him so his white mother's breast would stay up. He would say, in his own redneck way, that was why he was musical. "Chocolate milk! A hee, hee, hee."

His chucker Greely came into the room, someone who un-peopled individuals for Big Jim, the extricator that un-fouled situations that Big Jim considered a threat to his Piedmont empire in North Carolina.

"I think my best friend in Florida is suffering from drop foot or something."

"You talkin about AM?" Big Jim's man Greely said.

"And I think it's time we get the car and take a ride. We'll go over towards the coast to US 17. Take it to Jacksonville, where it kinda quits anyway, then do the rest on US 1 into Jensen Beach."

"Gonna take a lot longer."

"I hate the interstate. We'll do it like our Tar Heel brother Charles Kuralt would."

Big Jim was surprised to find Sermon feeding gopher tortoises and overseeing a work stoppage on the remaining area where the cockade woodpeckers lived. Big Jim was not happy about the land AM gave up to protect the two species, but then, Big Jim never woke up with a rotting bird staring him in the face, or a forty-grit hide land turtle in his bed. They went to lunch at The Blue Goose to talk things over.

"I sure do like this restaurant place, AM. You say it's been here a long time?"

"Yes, since the Twenties, I'm told," said AM, nervous. He knew Big Jim came for a reason and probably had a man working on the project to watch what went on.

"Just look at the wide river out there," Big Jim sang. "The barrier island on the other side reminds me of the rivers and islands along the Hatteras coast. Why, sittin out here on this porch is almost like being on a boat. Hear that water lappin under the floor? Look down through the cracks in the boards. You can actually see the river." Greely and AM nodded. "Was a great ride down on the US 1. Lot of old Florida left, old motels and fruit stands. Always know when I'm getting close to here cause we pass this stucco orange building in the actual shape of a giant orange in New Smyrna, I think it is. I mean, it's in the real shape of an orange, the whole building, or maybe it's in Eau Gallie. Where is it, Greely?"

Greely shook his head.

"Now what in the hell is going on at the project? I heard there's been some delays, vandalism, and changes of plans on the land you and I own together."

"Locals," AM said, looking for a whipping boy so Big Jim wouldn't try to make him his spaniel.

"I heard some wild-ass things occurred, some spooky animal disruption and destruction."

"Yes. The security guard who quit swore he saw a snake go by his post with its tail in its mouth, rolling like a hoop. He also claimed that an armadillo started a fire, and there were alligator tracks everywhere. That was after we had trouble with the pond depths. The ponds were dug too deep, and somebody or something penetrated the aquifer. He kept saying he thought the alligators did it."

"What? He crazy?"

"Maybe."

"Sounds like the vandal is running a cover and tryin to blame it on ole Spooky. Snake with its tail in its mouth? Shape of a hoop? Armadillo arsonist! It's the ole cold call hoo-doo. Come on, ya, AM. I know that one. My momma taught me that one."

Aubrey and Freddie Tommie came in for lunch. A couple of people stood when Aubrey walked by and shook his hand. AM pointed him out to Big Jim and Greely.

"There is one of my problems. The big fish, small pond man over there at that window table, and maybe that Indian with him. That Indian was seen leaving the area close to Cypress Prairie a couple of times. He applied for a job with the grounds people, but they wouldn't hire him. And the Indian is a good friend of the big fish, Aubrey Shallcross."

"Well, then, I bet you there's your spook. The Indian's makin trouble. Them Lumbees and Cherokee make trouble at home. Find out what you can about the Indian, Greely. See if he filled out a job application when he was on the project and look at it. Kill the son of a bitch, if you have to."

"No, Big Jim, you can't have him do that!"

"Now, now, AM, you didn't hear that. I'm just kiddin. Don't you worry about Greely. He's cunnin' and cold as the heart of an elderly whore, but he ain't gonna kill nobody. You get in touch with that Mr. Shallcross for a sit down while I'm here. I am not gonna let a bunch a tree worshippers screw us out of our investment here, and then we end up with a nothin' burger."

Three days later, Greely put together a rifle and scope from the trunk of the car and stuck a handgun in his belt. Freddie was with Claddy Nelson, working on a place. Greely waited for Claddy to leave for lunch. He walked up on Freddie in a stand of Brazilian peppers, and Freddie saw the look of him. The handgun came out. Freddie dodged the first shot behind a pepper tree, and then ran down a ditch toward a canal. The second bullet hit him in the top left of his upper back, but he kept running and dove into the canal, disappearing in some cattails. Greely stood on the bank. He saw an eight-foot gator in the water where Freddie went in, shrugged, and left him for dead. Freddie crawled out a half hour later and got back to Claddy. Claddy drove him to the hospital, Freddie struggling for breath. Deputy Kimmel had the hospital keep it secret, hoping the would-be killer would think Freddie was dead and stay in the area.

Aubrey went to see Freddie in the ICU. He could talk, but he was weak. Freddie gave Aubrey a description of Greely, who had one gold front tooth. Detective Kimmel interviewed Freddie, but Freddie was tight lipped about it. He wanted a private revenge. In the next days, Freddie and Aubrey talked about their lives to keep Freddie's mind off the pain of a collapsed lung. Freddie asked Aubrey where he came up with the name Drayton for his boy, and he told him it was his father's name. Then Aubrey asked Freddie how he named his son Yuchee.

"He is named after Uchee Billy, the chief of the lost Uchee Tribe, even though we spell it different, yes? They were a great tribe once in Tennessee and Alabama. They have disappeared now. The last of them fought with the Seminoles against Andrew Jackson. Uchee Billy was captured about the time Osceola was and went to prison in St. Augustine with him. He died in prison right before Osceola did, and guess what? They cut off his head for a trophy, like they did Osceola's, yes?"

Aubrey saw it. Both leaders desecrated, harvested for a conversation piece. He wondered if Uchee Billy's soul had found its way to someone or some creature like Two-Toed Tom, and if it did, what he was like.

"I'll get this guy who shot you, Freddie. *True* magazine, I will."

"No, Aubrey. I told you in the beginning, me or the big gators will do the killing. You only get in trouble. I am used to killing."

Aubrey had seen Sermon and friends twice at The Blue Goose for lunch. Greely, Big Jim's man, matched the description Freddie gave him, gold tooth pointing like a red arrow. Sermon contacted Aubrey for a peace talk, and they agreed to meet at the Goose for lunch on Wednesday.

Nemo was furious about Freddie getting shot. The House met at the campsite on the creek. It was a private meeting without Aubrey.

"I will exact payment for this, for my name is Nemo. In Latin, it means 'no man,' and I sit in judgment as no man. No man is the concept of the common law, the blindfold on the woman holding the Scales of Justice, and no man breaks that law without eventual punity. He offended mankind, this Greely – man's law, not nature's. It is hard to offend nature. Maybe impossible. But he did not kill for food or to protect himself; he killed for power and gain, meanness, the same thing I confronted with the war mongers in the 1800s, when they murdered my wife and child. I sailed the Nautilus under the oceans, looking for their galleons and war ships, sending them to the bottom. Yes, I am Nemo, and no man is allowed to do these things."

All sat in a determined silence.

On Tuesday morning, Aubrey sat with Christaine on the porch drinking coffee. "What are you going to say to Sermon? You think he'll try to bribe you or make a deal?" Christaine asked.

"All of the above, I guess," Aubrey said.

The phone rang. It was Sermon. "I must speak with you in private before Wednesday's lunch. My partner in the project, a major headache, insists on being at the meeting Wednesday. Will you meet me alone in an hour somewhere?"

"Okay, Sermon. How about the café on US 1? Randolph's?"

"Thank you. One hour."

They sat in a booth. Coffee in front of them. Sermon talked in a calm voice, but his shaking hands belied the calm. Aubrey let him talk without interruption. Sermon spoke of his recent conversion, like someone telling you about the day the Lord came into their life. Aubrey thought it might be a hustle, but Sermon's eyes were wet. He said Big Jim suggested harming the Indian, and he had made him promise no harm would come to anyone. "I went to college with the man. I knew his family was mostly illegal, but Big Jim seemed like he was not going to go that way. His father wanted Big Jim to be legitimate. Well, Mr. Shallcross, that went south, and he has become the worst of them. I want out. I want to change my life."

Aubrey just listened. Didn't mention what happened to Freddie. Sermon said he had come to realize he didn't like himself anymore. He said he planned to give the project to the county for a park; he had no son, no daughter to leave anything to, and of all things, he felt closer to the chimpanzee he had purchased from the carnival than any human being he knew.

"I heard you had Kong at your place. I didn't know what your intentions were with him."

"How about he inherits all my money?"

Aubrey stared across the table. They didn't speak. "You're serious, aren't you?" Aubrey said finally. "You'd really give that land to the county?"

Sermon nodded. "I just have to get Big Jim out of the deal."

"Can you afford to buy him out?"

"Not now. I am in trouble with the federal government for mail fraud. But one aspect of this whole deal at Cypress Prairie is fragile: Big Jim's money is dirty and being laundered through a bank in Canada. He feeds cash into the project and gets it cleaned when we pay bills with it, and then gets it back plus a profit as we sell the lots and houses. If I made a big enough fuss about leaving, Big Jim might back down for fear of his scheme being revealed. He wants no red flags. Of course, later he might have me killed."

Aubrey believed him. Sermon would never have told a secret like that, risking his life with Big Jim and bringing himself more trouble with the government, if he didn't want to change and give that land to the county.

"How bad is your problem with the government?"

"Bad. I'll probably take a plea deal. Then I'll be going away for a while."

"I see. What should we do about lunch with Big Jim tomorrow?"

"I will give my equity in the project away. My attorney says it'll look good to the judge when I'm up for sentencing for mail fraud, but that's not the reason I'm doing it. I tell you, Aubrey, I don't want it anymore. I'm haunted by it all. I want peace and to go away and then come back here and live peacefully. I am very fond of this place."

"Me, too." Aubrey smiled. "How about this? At lunch tomorrow, I'll offer to buy him out. I'll make some phone calls today and let well-heeled friends know this is possibly affordable, since you are donating your share. I won't tell them the details. We can then donate the land back to the county. My friends are philanthropic-minded and probably would like the write-off, along with the good feeling of giving the land back. A certain resource trust they are part of does these things, if these things are affordable. If you will truly donate your half, maybe Big Jim will give in and sell his part to the trust because you aren't going forward with the project. If so, this is doable."

"He's going be furious."

"He is responsible for having my friend Freddie Tommie shot. He is going to be okay, but I'm furious at him, AM."

AM stared, then shook his head when Aubrey told him about Freddie. He told Aubrey he was so sorry.

Sermon went home that day and sat with his only comfort – Kong, the prize fighter. He talked to Kong for an hour. Kong would look at him, look away, then look at him again. When Sermon started to cry, Kong reached out and touched him with the back of his hairy hand.

Aubrey went home and talked to his Christaine. They both were amazed by the pirouette Sermon had made.

At noon the next day, Aubrey went through the doors of The Blue Goose. The other party was already seated on the river porch. Sermon introduced him to Big Jim and Greely, but no one shook hands. Aubrey sat, and all the perfunctory pleasantries of a first encounter began to flow from Big Jim's southern mouth.

He asked Aubrey about the area and the restaurant. Then Roberta and Speedy came in, Roberta in her wheelchair. Aubrey nodded to them, surprised, with "Come on over" eyes, but they moved past him to a table in the corner.

"Now what? Aubrey's sitting with them," Speedy said to Roberta.

"Can't stop it, Speedy. You just have to be in the right place to protect him when it happens."

Speedy nodded. Roberta stuck her hand in her purse to signal the coach whip and Roy, its slipper. The snake slid out of the bag and to the floor, moving along the baseboards, around stations of restaurant equipment, Roy driving. He slipped the snake through a hole in the floor boards and wove through cross bracing in the joists below, until he was exactly beneath the table where Sermon and the rest of the party sat. The snake slid through an oversized cutout of an electrical outlet under the table, until it was staring at the men's feet. Roy left a long section of the snake's tail hanging down below the floor to mark the spot.

The Dragon and Two-Toed Tom swam three feet under the surface in the Indian River, coming up with their noses to grab air then re-submerging. When they were under the dock that ran out from the porch of The Blue Goose, they came up between the pilings, unseen. Nemo and Osceola walked out on the noses of their redoubtable reptiles. Nemo shook Osceola's hand, and they nodded and went back into their gators' minds to sit in their eyes and continue the mission. Two-Toed swam along the dock pilings and under the restaurant until the water was only a foot deep. The Dragon went around to a floating dock on the side that was barely above the water line.

Two-Toed saw the tail of the coach whip marking the location of the table. Roy moved the snake out of the way. Nemo waited outside for what he knew would be a loud noise. Just then, Freddie Tommie came in with a limp and approached the table. Freddie wore a traditional Seminole shirt, patterned in red, black, and gold, the tribe's colors. Greely's face fell. He slowly reached for his gun as Two-Toed set his muscular tail and hind legs in the sand below and shot through the floor boards in a convulsion of power and violence. Splinters and boards flying, he grabbed Greely's legs with his steel trap mouth.

Greely screamed, "Oh, God! Oh, God, no."

Freddie leaned closer and locked onto Greely's eyes but did not touch him. Greely started to raise his gun hand, and Roy sent the coach whip. The snake wrapped around the hand and bit Greely in the face. At the same time, The Dragon crashed into the room from the side door and let Martha and her snake out of his mouth, then grabbed Big Jim by the legs. Speedy jumped to his feet and dragged Aubrey away from the struggle. Aubrey brought Sermon with him.

Speedy tried to make Aubrey let go of Sermon so the gators could have him, but Aubrey had Sermon under the arms and dragged him further away. The patrons could only watch. There were tables blocking the one path off the porch to the main part of the restaurant, which was safely on solid land.

Big Jim and Greely continued to scream like two Robert Shaws sliding into the shark's jaws in front of Roy Scheider and Richard Dreyfuss. It made some people look away, the blood spurting, even Aubrey, but Freddie Tommie stood close and never took his eyes off it.

The last and worst part was watching Big Jim and Greely pulled through the hole in the floor Two-Toed had opened, their hands and nails scraping along the wood until they were under the porch. Still they screamed in the shallow water, as the crowd turned towards the river to see the men kicking and flailing before the gators swam further out then dove, and started their butchering spins.

There were no sirens yet. There was crying and consolation. How could anyone in The Blue Goose describe what they saw that day? Aubrey looked at Speedy and Freddie and shook his head. "What-what is this?"

Speedy pulled Aubrey to him and said, "The plan was not to tell you, Aubrey. No one wanted you blamed or charged with any of this, especially Freddie."

"But what about you, Speedy?"

"Roberta and I were just here for lunch. Freddie was meeting us, but he was a little late."

Freddie looked at Aubrey, smiling, "I don't drive as fast lately. Takes me longer to get somewhere. Yes?" Then Freddie sneaked a hand in his pocket and dropped a small piece of colored Seminole cloth by the hole in the floor.

Roberta motioned to Speedy to come over. "Where are the snakes?"

Speedy looked down. "Under the table, waiting for you to let them in your tote bag."

Sermon was in shock. Aubrey sat in a chair next to him and said, "I had no idea. All I can say is that this is the world of *animale*, a world you are getting to know lately. You can't offend nature. Or can you, AM?"

Sermon shook his head, trying to purchase the meaning of Aubrey's words as the cops pulled in.

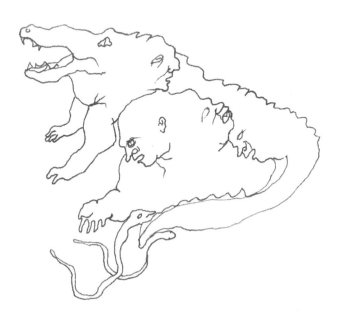

Chapter 32: THE TIN SNIP KILLER

A month later, after the national press had licked the place bare, each of the friends sometimes stopped in the middle of something to return to that day. Another thing happened a month after The Blue Goose incident, something that would sit in the same corner of their thoughts for the rest of their lives.

They all went to Nell's new place on the creek to help her clean it up. They saw a man swimming across from the other side, and when he stood on the bottom to walk out of the water, it turned out to be Half Track, the gone-minded brother from the Harris Ranch.

At first, he just sat on the ground shaking his head. Then he said, "Secret. Secret." Aubrey asked him what secret. "Sonny said secret, secret. Sonny said secret." Half Track stood, walked over to a grassy spot that seemed like the rest of the ground and looked at his feet, still saying, "Secret. Secret."

When he started stomping the ground, pointing, Aubrey got a shovel. He, Arquette, and John Chrome took turns digging until the rusting white of a refrigerator door showed three feet down. Half Track got louder – Rain Man louder. "Secret! Secret!" he yelled, looking back at Sonny's old trailer. Aubrey opened the door of the buried appliance and there, in the long awaited light, was a dried, skin-wrapped skeleton with a milky plastic breathing mask still on its eye-socket face. The tube from the mask ran to a small metal bottle with a fading label that read Freon. Beside the body were a pair of handcuffs and two 8x10 glass-framed photographs, one of Aubrey, Sonny, and The Junior in front of the bookstore, and one of Nell and her aunt. A ship in a bottle, the Charles W. Morgan whaler, lay on its side by Sonny's chest. There was an envelope in the pocket of the rotted shirt. It was another copy of Sonny's will, leaving Nell everything, in case they found his body before he was declared legally dead. And finally, one mummified hand cradled a pair of tin snips. They had found him, the Tin Snip Killer. It was Sonny all along. Nell fainted. Aubrey wanted to drive Half Track home, but instead he ran to the water crying and swam for the other side.

Deputy Kimmel had the whole place excavated and the creek bottom dragged with grappling hooks. They found Sonny's big Freon tanks in the creek, and other old refrigerators buried on the property full of evidence. One had another body in it.

Chapter 33: WELTANSCHUUANG: THE WAY ONE SEES THE WORLD, AND THEIR PLACE IN IT.

I've been thinking about novels – me, Charles Porter – their elements, points of view, irony, ambiguity, surrealism, metaphor, meta-metaphor, especially ambiguity. In the *Shallcross* book, the Blue Goose bunch tried to get the meaning of the bumper sticker on Punky's dump truck: **Jesus Paid for Our Sins, Now Let's Get Our Money's Worth.** Does that mean we get to sin because it has been paid for, or does it mean we have to behave now, because of what Jesus did for us? **You Can't Offend Nature** is a bumper sticker just as ambiguous as the Jesus one. Does it mean you better not offend nature, or it can't be done? Nemo thinks you can offend it in a certain way, and the Seminoles think you can, because to them the bumper sticker means you better not.

And I've been thinking about Sonny – how one of his victims was a man who butchered veal calves for a living. He put the man's Freon-filled body in an old refrigerator and wrote on the door in his blood, "He Offended Nature," but did he? Is the behavior of everything just natural?

I wonder about the killing and eating of babies – lamb chops, calves' livers, baby back ribs, eggs, bug larva. In *Flame Vine*, it was said, "We eat the young of everything, and so does everything else. In fact, we, me, and the kingdom animale go out of our way to get them."

And I've been thinking about that old aria of rotting compost they call God and religion, that pile that invented morality and decided some of this stuff that happens is offensive, how this pile wants us *not* to offend each other unless it's for Him upstairs and the pile, how this morality is supposed to save us. How absurd this must look to the natural laws of the universe, as it kills stars and planets and makes new ones. How absurd we must appear to the quantum doo lang laws of the cosmos on this cloudy little pellet, this BB stuck in the back of a small drawer inside an expanding mansion of galaxy after galaxy. I don't think you can offend nature. It's much too big and powerful. We only offend ourselves and our chances of survival.

That day, Aubrey stood on the high deck of his house looking at all the land he owned and said, "Is this my empire? No. I am my empire. My head is my mansion." Triple Suiter heard him and told him to come down and, "Stop fingering the finery."

We *have* fingered the finery. Alligators will outlive us. The water is coming.

CODA

Mary Kincaid, the euthanasia veterinarian shot in the foot by Shane Richards a year ago, is back on the road to provide Peace for Pets, only now she's licensed to carry. Oh, yeah.

At the *Washington Post*, a reporter says, "Something's fishy," while she sits and wonders what the hell really went on in that small South Florida town with those murdering alligators. Oh, yeah.

In a den under the creek bank, Osceola and Two-Toed Tom take a parting look at the embosomed human heads and skulls they have along a sandy wall, then swim south for the Everglades with Nemo and The Dragon to hide out for a while. Oh, yeah.

In the cottage Nell rented from Aubrey, she and Freddie make love for the first time and laugh about having softer bodies at their age to cushion the blows. Oh, yeah.

John Chrome sits and wonders why Levon's child Jesus left Levon in that Elton John song and went to Venus to fly balloons while Levon slowly dies. Chrome thinks that's the reason he decided not to have children. Oh, yeah.

In a federal prison, AM sits for mail fraud looking at a picture on his cell wall of Marjorie Stoneman Douglas, the famous Florida environmentalist. Yesterday, before they put him in handcuffs, he kissed an ape on the head after leaving him a trust fund, and said he'd see him in two years. He donated all his Florida land to the county for a preserve. Oh, yeah.

Leda was right. When Sonny's body was completely exhumed, they found the faded word MIDGE tattooed on his arm in honor of Thomas Midgley, who invented Freon. Oh, yeah.

In a summer Ohio town, Speedy flies around, upside down, in the Globe of Death, high as Gilderoy, while Roberta still wows the crowds with her marvelous snake act. Oh, yeah.

On a back road west of town, Henry the taxidermist is releasing baby rattlesnakes in the woods and snail kites to hunt baby pythons. Oh, yeah.

At his old house on the Indian River, Arquette throws up every morning when he wonders what he's doing here, and at night takes a pull on a nitrous oxide bottle to slip away. Oh, yeah.

At Aubrey and Christaine's, Drayton and Yuchee Tommie play in the yard together on weekends. One day, when they are old enough, they will forge an eco-alliance that will shake the government to the bone around Lake Okeechobee, I promise. Oh, yeah.

And Aubrey sits on the side of the road in the tabernacle of his truck. The big grocery haulers go by with signs on their sides that say Moon Pie, Sara Lee, Nut Harvest, Tide, and most, most personal, Arm and Hammer. He wonders for a moment if these signs are the new Bible, until the sound of their Jake brakes go budadddddda, down to an exit taking him to the no-fly zone. Oh, yeah.

FINISHED

INTERVIEW

A Conversation with J. North Conway and Charles Porter

J. North Conway (Jack Conway) is the author of more than a dozen books. His most recent, *The Wreck of the Portland*, was published in 2019. He is also the author of a trilogy about New York City during the gilded age that includes the *King of Heists*, hailed by the Wall Street Journal as one of the best books of summer 2009. He is the recipient of the John Curtis Award for Lifelong Learning.

JNC: Have you moved into fantasy with this third book in your series? You said in your other two, "This is all taken from the real world, nothing is supernatural or fantasy."

CP: I think fantasy is when a creature, human, or animal, can lift a car over their head. My creatures only perform realistic feats. Except for the armadillo, who can strike his toenails together, make a spark and start a fire; that could be a stretch. As far as slippers like Nemo and Osceola go in this story, it is not unusual for someone to think they have a spiritual companion or to think that certain animals behave like they have a human inside them, nothing in the story changes into another unnatural creature and there is nothing supernatural about a hallucination.

JNC: What are slippers, the characters in your books—Triple Suiter, Amper Sand, Nemo, the noumenon you called them from the Greek word *noomenon* if I remember, that which is apprehended only by thought, not the exterior senses.

CP: Slippers? Everyone has them in their head. Kant said they are forms that can be known to exist, but to which no normal outside properties can be ascribed. Slippers are inaccessible to outside phenomenal experience for most people. Those people see and hear them only in dreams, dreams from that un-locatable location of things thought about. But they are more substantial than that for people who have bicameral minds, voice hearers and seers, western society unfortunately calls schizophrenics.

JNC: Why do you say it's unfortunate that people use that word schizophrenic?

CP: It's old code for crazy. There is a worldwide organization, The Hearing Voices Network, that eschews that word and prefers those people be referred to as simply voice hearers. And if you are one of those people in other cultures like Africa or South America, you would be considered close to divine.

JNC: Back to slippers. In the other interviews you called them a, "mostly unknown segment of existence."

CP: Yes, the other more paraded *known* segments of existence are, heaven, hell, a parallel universe, and Plato's shadow world, no one talks about slippers except the talk walkers; science says they are just hallucinations. I think slippers are us after we die, revenants that live in our minds and the minds of other living things because that's where we choose to live after we lose the corporeal state we once occupied.

JNC: This book is more about slippers that occupy animals than people.

CP: They can move into anything living thing if they want to. They transport through the breath and the nose when people or animals get close enough to each other. But I think they like living in the minds of people mostly, because the human is what they used to be, however living in a buzzard for a while and flying five thousand feet off the earth is as Triple Suiter once put it, "The Cadillac of the slip away."

JCN: How did you pick alligators for this story?

CP: I know alligators. I grew up handling and hunting the things. I could make that guttural gator sound they make in my throat when I was nine years old. The men in the family would put me in the bow of an airboat at night and have me watch for stumps when we hunted. Airboats can even go across dry land if there is enough dew. We would hunt where the water was sometimes only a foot deep, and a log, or a stump, can open the bottom of a boat going thirty miles and hour like a can opener.

JNC: This is in South Florida?

CP: Yes, the backwoods and wetlands of Palm Beach and Martin County on the east coast.

JNC: You were hunting them for the hides?

CP: Yes, in the 1950's, when I was a kid, hides were going for around $7.00 a foot, which we thought was a lot of money considering a ranch foreman's salary was only $100.00 a week back then, and the gators were just as plentiful as they are today. They're very prolific. It was illegal to hunt them. Today they have commercial farms that raise them for the hides and meat, but today there are still 1.3 million wild alligators in the state of Florida. They are everywhere and very dangerous.

JNC: Ever have any close calls?

CP: Not hunting. Gators get people when they do stupid things; when they are distracted by something, I took more risks when I swam in ponds at night with my girlfriends as nature made me. That's distracted. That could have been like the opening scene in *Jaws*.

JNC: What else about the gator hunting as a boy?

CP: The hides were salted, rolled, and tied with baling twine. On Thursdays we'd go to the cattle auction in Okeechobee and take three or four steers in a cattle truck. We put a foot and a half of sawdust in the bed of the truck for the steers to stand on, deeper than usual you know, and under there and the cow shit would be the rolled up gator hides.

We'd drop off the steers and keep going towards the Peace River where we'd meet a hide buyer and sell them the goods. It was sort of like a drug deal in a way. The grownups figured if we were stopped, no lawman in their nice dry-cleaned shirts would want to dig though urine soaked sawdust with cow shit everywhere looking for things.

JNC: Back to books. Do you read non-fiction?

CP: Sure. Interesting though, I saw that Bill Gates, Warren Buffet, and Elon Musk, said they only read non-fiction and self-help books for recreation, and the person who wrote the article made a point of saying all three men said they don't read novels.

JNC: What do you think of that?

CP: I read nonfiction and novels. I love stories, true ones, historical ones, exaggerated true ones, and totally made up ones. I'm very interested in narrators and especially narrators in stories that slip into character, what's known as a reliably unreliable narrator. We are all narrators, even Gates, Buffet, Musk, but I think people who don't read novels, who purposely exclude them, are missing out on that kind of introspection and surprise the novel wakes in a person. Makes you wonder what's happened to some forms of creative thinking in the last fifty years. Everyday thought today can be a lot of mid brain, where the appetites live, I mean that's part of life too, and I do it, but I think the appetites get a stronger lift after the big cortex behind the forehead has had a burst, what Milan Kundera calls, "The suddenly kindled light of the never before seen." I really like to read and write about things that aren't there, that weren't ever there, until suddenly written, or suddenly filmed, or suddenly shaped. That blows me away. That's mansion.

JNC: And so that's what you think of readers today?

CP: Of course not all of them, but what level does most of the country read on? I think of it like architecture: I didn't know I lived in a two-story house until I was fifteen years old. My brain I mean. Books sent me up the stairs. I didn't know my brain had a second story. There is a part in *Shallcross*, the first book, Trip is telling Aubrey, "Most people are not like you Aubrey, they don't know they have a second story, they live in a one story house; some don't even get past the foyer." Readers can be like that, so can film fans, most read one story books and go to one story films, but of course there is something to be said for Sheryl Crow's song line, "If it makes you happy, it can't be that bad." Suspect of course, I mean stupid is that bad, and dope is too, especially when it kills you, then I guess it is that bad. Anyway what I'm saying is, the demand for two story books, and especially those with an attic, is quite small it seems today. Do you think I'm a snob for saying that?

JNC: Yep.

CP: Me too.

JNC: Where do you see yourself in the literary world?

CP: Maybe country music. I don't think low school would read me, don't think the genuine high brows would either, but maybe, if it makes them happy, so back to Sheryl Crow again.

JNC: Who would you like to read you?

CP: Um, musicians. I love music. Lately, Nick Cave that fronts for that band The Bad Seeds, he wrote a weird book, *The Death of Bunny Munro*, I'd like him to read me; or Rye Cooder the slide guitarist, or Ferry Lewis another slide man where Rye mopped licks. Of course Ferry's dead now, and he came from the deep south. I don't know if he even *could* read, something adulterous about it if he could. And the writers, there's so many I like: Annie Proulx, I admire her and her stuff; she's a mansion, and James Wood, the book critic for *The New Yorker*, I really like his take on books and authors.

JNC: As a joke, because you and I like to laugh, I'm going to ask that awful question going around lately, "What books are on your nightstand, and believe me my tongue is in my cheek?"

CP: I know, I know, everybody asks that interview question, but you and I do like to laugh, Jack. I saw you stick your tongue in your cheek. The truth is, only film is on my nightstand – DVD's, no books. Most writers I bet when they get in bed from working all day, maybe there's a book next to a glass of water and a bottle of Tums, I don't know, but for sure there's a big Samsung screen at the end of the bed. I watch film at night. I don't want to read anything after reading all day.

JNC: What else Charlie? How about that old saying in your book, "You can't offend nature," a little haunting isn't it? Do you think it's true?

CP: It's true, and at the same time it's not. I remember my grandmother used to always say, "Let nature take its course." When you think about that, it's both wonderful and awful, classic terrible and sublime. I mean when nature takes its course, it can also be a horror show watching us and every other living thing on this hostile planet. Of course nature doesn't think it's a horror show, it just thinks that's nature, and you, I mean us, as this book says, "Can't offend it," it's too damn big. We only offend ourselves.

JNC: And you put down a warning in one chapter, "Don't finger the finery," your slipper, Triple Suiter, said that, and I think you're right, we have fingered the finery and because we have, the last line in your book is somewhat of a javelin, "The water is coming." Better leave it at that, you think?

CP: Yep. The water is coming. Let's leave it at that. Thanks for talking with me Jack.

THE HEARING VOICES SERIES

SHALLCROSS

The Blindspot Cathedral   A NOVEL

"Surreal, poetic, and unforgettable:
a truly original voice."

KIRKUS REVIEWS

"Unfailingly original..."

BLUEINK REVIEWS

Charles Porter

Made in the USA
Middletown, DE
06 August 2020